Saving Apollo

By Charles Huss

For my wife, Rose, who has put up with me for over twenty-five years and still wants more.

Chapter 1

Charles Jones opened the heavy metal door and stepped inside the lab. The smell of bleach irritated his nose just as the sound of several barking dogs overwhelmed his ears. He hated coming to the lab, but after avoiding it for months, he felt he needed to check on his investment. He walked past rows of cages stacked three high on both sides. Each housed a single animal. There were rats, rabbits, guinea pigs, and various other mammals. There were no birds, reptiles, or amphibians, just mammals. He then came upon at least a dozen large pens occupied by dogs. There were German Shepherds, Labradors, and Dobermans. Each door had a nameplate with the name of a Greek god or goddess printed on it. As he passed, the remaining dogs started barking.

Dr. Kevin Miller and his grad student assistant, Jenny Smith, were in the center of the room where they had set up a makeshift obstacle course. Miller, in his early thirties, was young for his position. He stood just under six feet tall with short, thick brown hair parted neatly on the side.

In her early twenties, Jenny was of average height and had long, dishwater-blonde hair tied in a ponytail. Her soft features and warm smile conveyed a girl-next-door charm.

A young but nearly full-grown Doberman stood beside Jenny and Dr. Miller. He watched as Charles Jones approached.

"Anything new to report?" Jones asked.

"Oh, yes, Mr. Jones. All the dogs in our study have shown some cognitive improvements, but this one here, Apollo, and his sister, Athena, have exceeded all expectations," Miller said.

"So, what can this dog do?" Jones asked.

"Well, for one thing, he's good at understanding spoken English. I don't mean commands. I mean actual sentences."

"You mean he can understand what we are discussing right now?"

"Maybe not our entire conversation, but certainly some of it. He's still learning. The more time he spends with a person, the better he understands them. The same goes for Athena. They become familiar with a person's speech patterns. It would be similar to a young child understanding their parents better than a stranger. You could give them instructions, and they would probably know at a basic level what you want, but if I tell them something, it is almost certain that they will understand. Also, I'm familiar with which words they have learned so far, and I'm careful to use words they know."

"This is more than I expected. If you are correct, these dogs and those that follow will help humans in ways never thought possible. Our stock price will go through the roof. Of course, we must first prove their effectiveness. It will be a game-changer if they can understand instructions that will change based on the situation."

"I'm very hopeful," Miller said. "I think they will be perfect for the job, but while they are young and learning, the instructions should come from their handler or someone they know well and who knows them well. I believe they will improve and be able to understand anyone over time. Once Apollo and Athena are fully mature, we will better understand what they are truly capable of."

Jones thought momentarily and said, "It would be great if they could understand everyone, but even understanding a single person would be more than adequate. Can you show me an example?"

"Sure. Jenny, can you put the ropes down?"

Jenny grabbed three ropes of different lengths and put them on the floor in front of Apollo. Dr. Miller put a knee on the ground, placed his hand on Apollo's shoulder, and said, "Apollo, please bring me the shortest rope."

Apollo walked to the ropes, found the shortest one, picked it up, and returned it to Dr. Miller.

"That's good," Jones said, "but I have seen better tricks from normal dogs."

Miller patted Apollo on the head and said, "Now, get the longest rope and bring it to Jenny."

Apollo picked up the long rope and brought it to Jenny, who said, "Good boy, Apollo. Now, pick up the last rope, walk three steps forward, then drop it."

Apollo picked up the last rope, took three steps forward, then dropped it.

"Now I'm impressed," Jones said. "Did you practice that with him?"

"Yes and no," Miller said. "We change the order and number of steps, so it's never the same twice."

"Can the other one do the same things?"

"Oh yes," Miller said. "We haven't even scratched the surface of what they can both do."

"Show me more," Jones said.

"Sure, Mr. Jones. Jenny, bring out Athena, please."

Jenny left and returned with Athena, who sat beside Apollo.

"Jenny, get the balls, please," Miller said.

Jenny retrieved a painter's bucket, removed ten balls, and placed them on the floor.

Miller said, "Athena, bring me four balls. Apollo, bring me three balls."

The two dogs each picked up a ball and dropped them at Miller's feet. They returned, picked up another ball each, and dropped them at Miller's feet. When each dog dropped the appropriate number of balls, they sat and waited for their next instruction.

"That's incredible," Jones said. "How high can they count?"

"So far, we have only tested them to ten, but I suspect they can go considerably higher," Miller said.

"What about colors?" Jones asked.

"That's a little trickier. Dogs have a dichromatic vision, meaning they can only see blues and yellows. Reds appear dark or black, and colors that have red in them appear more subdued to them. To answer your question, they know the difference between blue and yellow."

"What about their ability to solve problems?" Jones asked.

"I think to demonstrate that, we need to do something that we haven't practiced," Miller said. "Let me think. Oh, I know."

Miller picked up a broom and unscrewed the handle. He placed the handle on the floor near a tunnel they used for training. He then asked Jenny to stand on the other side of the tunnel. He knelt beside Athena, pointed at the broom handle, and said, "Bring the stick to Jenny."

Athena walked to the broom handle, picked it up, and then realized it would not fit through the tunnel, so she walked around the tunnel and dropped it at Jenny's feet.

Miller clapped and said, "Very good, Athena," as he walked over and picked up the handle. He placed it back down in front of the tunnel and said, "Okay, Athena, now bring the stick through the tunnel to Jenny."

Athena walked over to the broom handle, thought for a moment, then picked it up from one end and kept her head turned to the right as she walked into the tunnel. The other end dragged along the ground as she made her way through the tunnel and deposited the broom handle in front of Jenny again. Jenny hugged her and said, "Very good, Athena. You're a smart girl."

"Okay, I've seen enough," Jones said. "I'm going to arrange a meeting with a potential client as soon as possible, so be ready."

"Yes, sir, Mr. Jones. We'll be ready," Miller said.

As Charles Jones was leaving, all the dogs started barking again. "Shut up, you mangy mutts!" he yelled before leaving the lab.

"That guy gives me the willies, Kevin," Jenny said after the door closed.

"I know what you mean. I love what I do here, but sometimes regret taking this job."

Kevin Miller opened a drawer and took out a bag of dog treats. He gave some to Athena and Apollo and said, "Thank you both for putting up with Mr. Grumpy."

Both dogs barked simultaneously, and he patted them on the head.

When Charles Jones returned to his office, he picked up the phone and dialed a number. When it was answered, he said, "General Adams, this is Charles Jones from CJL. Our dogs are ready for a demonstration whenever you are."

Chapter 2

Twelve-year-old Ethan was playing a video game on his phone when his father tapped him on the shoulder and said, "We're here."

Ethan looked up and saw they were driving over a bridge. At the end of the bridge was a sign saying, "Welcome to Pelican Pointe."

"That's good," he said, returning to his game.

"I want you to see this, Ethan. This is old-world Florida. Most of these barrier islands have been taken over by high-rise condominiums, but this is real beauty here.

"Yeah, it's nice, Dad," Ethan said without looking up.

Ethan's dad shook his head in frustration. After a couple of minutes, the moving truck they were following stopped on the street in front of their new home. He parked behind them and got out of the car. The truck driver got out, too. He was a tall, muscular man wearing a T-shirt that seemed two sizes too small. "Mr. Clark, somebody's parked in your driveway," the man said.

It was a modest-sized home built on tall pilings that overlooked the Gulf of Mexico. A stairway led up the center of the house to the front door. There was enough room under the home to park two vehicles. There was no beach; mangrove trees separated the home from the water. A white Ford Explorer was parked at the end of the narrow driveway near the street. A similar home stood to the left. To the right was an empty lot.

"Just a minute," he said to the driver and headed to the house on the left. He climbed the stairs and knocked on the door.

A young woman holding a bowl of cereal answered the door. She looked like she had just rolled out of bed. She wore an oversized T-shirt with what looked like pajama bottoms. Her long, auburn red hair was a mess, but her deep green eyes were mesmerizing.

"Hi. Um, my name is, uh, I'm Ryan Clark. I'm your new neighbor. I bought the house next door. Is that your car in my driveway?"

The woman looked and said, "Oh, yes. I'm sorry. I didn't realize the house was sold. My name is Brooke, by the way. Brooke McCabe."

"I'm very pleased to meet you, Brooke."

She ran her fingers through her hair and said, "I'll move the car. Give me a minute."

She went back inside and closed the door. Ryan walked back to his property and waited. Five minutes later, Brooke came out wearing a pair of tight jean shorts. She still wore the same T-shirt and hadn't combed her hair. Ryan wondered what she was doing for so long. "I'm sorry," she said again as she reached the driveway. It was raining yesterday when I got home, and my driveway gets muddy when it rains. I've been meaning to get it paved, but haven't gotten around to it yet."

She moved her car to her own driveway, and when she got out, she waved and said, "Nice meeting you, Ryan."

Ryan waved back and watched her until she disappeared into her house.

The moving guys worked for two hours, bringing all their belongings into the house. After they left, Ryan and Ethan spent the rest of the afternoon unpacking. Ryan called and ordered a pizza after they unpacked all the essential stuff. When it arrived, they sat on the sofa and ate. They were both exhausted.

"When is the cable going to be hooked up, Dad?" Ethan asked.

"Someone should be here Monday morning. Are you going through television withdrawal already?"

"Well, it's boring sitting here looking at a blank screen."

"What would you be doing if this were a hundred years ago, when nobody had a television to watch?"

"The same thing I'm doing now. Nothing."

"You need to go outside and make friends," Ryan said. "You can't spend your entire life inside watching television and playing video games."

"I had friends before you decided to move."

"You had one friend and a few acquaintances. The whole lot of you spent your time holed up in one house or another playing video games. That's not a life."

"What about you? You spend every day typing away at your computer. When do you go out to make friends?"

"I'm a writer, Ethan. I'm doing my job. It's what pays the bills. Although I suppose you're right. I should get out more. If we finish unpacking tomorrow, I'll make some time next week to do something fun. Maybe we can find something interesting to do on the island.

"Okay. Whatever."

Chapter 3

Monday morning, Kevin Miller and Jenny Smith stood outside, waiting for the meeting with investors that Charles Jones arranged. Between them sat Apollo and Athena. They were in a large, fenced-in area behind the main building. They had set up several obstacles for demonstration purposes. Head of security, Jack Strauss, stood at the far end of the fenced-in area, tranquilizer gun at the ready. A former Marine, Jack still sported a Marine haircut ten years after leaving the service. He had a handsome, rugged look, like the leading actor in an action movie.

Even though it was still early, it was already uncomfortably warm, and the air felt thick and heavy, like being covered by a wet blanket. It didn't help that there was no breeze.

Charles Jones entered the gate, followed by two Army officers wearing fatigues. He led them to Miller and Smith and said, "This is Dr. Kevin Miller, the project leader, and his assistant, Jenny Smith." He then pointed to the officers and said, "This is General Martin Adams, and this is Captain Brenda Davis."

They all shook hands, and Miller said, "Wait a minute. Are you here to turn my creations into war dogs?"

"You're out of line, Dr. Miller," Jones said. "These dogs could save lives in a combat mission."

"He's right," the General said. "We've been using dogs for a hundred years with great success. Having highly intelligent dogs on the front lines will mean even more soldiers will return to their families."

"Don't get me wrong, General," Miller said. "I have a high level of respect for you and all military members, but I designed these dogs to be perfect service dogs. They are here to help civilians, including veterans who need extra help after returning to civilian life. Combat was never something I considered when creating them. Besides, it won't be long before you have robots on the front lines. You won't need dogs or even people anymore."

"Maybe, Dr. Miller, but that time has not yet come," the General said.

"I will not participate in sending these dogs off to die on the other side of the world when they could be so much more useful here at home. I'm sorry, but I won't do it."

"Need I remind you who you are working for?" Jones snapped.

"As of right now, I'm working for nobody," Miller said before heading for the gate.

Jenny looked shocked at the development and wasn't sure what to do. She noticed everyone looking at her. She wanted to run and catch up with Dr. Miller, but needed the job. In the end, she did nothing.

General Adams looked at Jones and said, "Well, I guess it's back to the drawing board for you."

"This is just a temporary setback. Give me a little time, and I will get someone in here who thinks the way we do."

"Okay, Mr. Jones. If the dogs are as good as you say, they are worth waiting for, but only if you can get your people under control."

After the General and the Captain left the training area, Jones grabbed Athena and Apollo by their collars and said, "C'mon, let's go."

They didn't move.

"Let's go!" he said louder, pulling harder on their collars.

Upon seeing this, Jack Strauss started walking towards them like he expected trouble.

Jenny said, "I wouldn't do that, Mr. Jones."

"Nonsense!" Jones said. "These creatures need to be taught who the boss is. That's something that you will need to learn." With that, he pulled harder and dragged Apollo and Athena across the ground.

Apollo suddenly sprang forward, surprising Jones and breaking free of his grip. He raced to the gate, but the latch was too high. He jumped several times, attempting to flip the latch, but he didn't have the leverage while in the air.

"Shoot him!" Jones yelled to Strauss, who pulled out his tranquilizer gun and pointed it at Apollo. Just then, Athena twisted herself out of Jones's grip and threw herself against Strauss's arm. The gun flew out of his hand and hit the ground several feet away.

Athena picked up the gun and raced to the gate. Apollo saw that she was free and put his feet apart and his head down. When Athena reached him, she dropped the gun, climbed onto Apollo's back, and pushed the latch open. They both ran out of the gate with Jones and Strauss in pursuit. Jones picked up the gun, pointed at the parking lot, and said, "Take the Jeep."

There was a Jeep convertible in the parking lot that Strauss sometimes used to patrol the grounds and for occasional errands. The top was down, so Jones jumped into the passenger seat and stood up so he could shoot in any direction.

A ten-foot fence surrounded the entire property. The only way in or out was through a gate controlled by a security guard. Apollo and Athena reached the gate just after the General's car went through. They slipped past the gate as it closed.

"Open the gate! Open the gate!" Jones yelled as they approached. The guard hit the button, and the gate seemed to open at a snail's pace. When it was open far enough for the Jeep to squeeze through, Strauss put his foot all the way down on the accelerator. After thirty seconds, they saw the dogs racing down the side of the road. Apollo was in the lead and veered off toward the woods as the car approached. Jones managed to get off a shot before they disappeared into the trees.

The dart hit Athena in the side. Apollo wasn't aware that anything was wrong until he heard Athena bark a minute later. He turned around and saw her lying on the ground. He raced back to help her. He saw the dart sticking out of her side when he reached her. He pulled it out and licked her face. She licked him back before losing consciousness. Apollo barked but got no response from Athena. He heard the snap of a twig and looked up. Two men approached. He barked again, but still no response.

When Jones was free of obstructions, he took aim at Apollo and fired. The shot hit him on his left shoulder. Apollo knew he didn't have much time. He raced to find a good hiding place. He came out of the woods near a gas station. He could feel the drowsiness taking over, but forced himself to fight it. He saw several people pumping gas into their vehicles. An old pickup truck caught his eye. The gate was down, and a dirt bike stood in the center with four straps holding it in place. Apollo jumped into the truck's bed and curled up in front of the bike, hidden from view. He quickly fell asleep.

The pickup truck driver finished pumping gas and drove away just before Jones and Strauss came out of the woods. They looked around. Seeing no sign of Apollo, Jones said, "We can't let this dog fall into the hands of our competitors."

Strauss just nodded, and the two men walked back to their vehicle.

***

Apollo woke up about an hour later. He could tell the vehicle he was in wasn't moving, but where was he? He could feel the dart was still stuck in his shoulder, but couldn't reach it, so he stood up and shook himself as he would after a bath. That dislodged it. He then looked around to get his bearings. There were buildings all around him, as well as several parked cars. In front of the truck was a large window with a picture of a woman carrying a plate of food. That reminded him that he needed to find something to eat. He saw no people on the street. A large vehicle headed his way, so he waited until it passed and then jumped to the ground.

Apollo walked around to the back of the building and found a dumpster. The smell of meat wafted through the air, but the top of the dumpster was out of his reach. He looked around and spotted a five-gallon bucket. He tipped the bucket over and rolled it next to the dumpster. He flipped it upside down and pushed it to the proper distance. He then backed up, ran toward the bucket, and used it as a springboard to propel himself to the top of the dumpster. Once there, he used his nose to flip up the left side of the cover.

The trash was piled almost to the top, and flies buzzed around him as his nose attempted to locate where the smell was coming from. He pushed away some papers and found a large bone with plenty of meat still on it. He wondered why anyone would discard so much food. He picked up the bone and jumped to the ground. He brought the tasty treat to the back of the dumpster, where nobody could see him, and devoured the remainder of the steak.

When Apollo got all the meat off the bone that he could, he started walking. He didn't know where he was going or who he could trust. He thought it best to stay out of sight as much as possible, although that wasn't easy. Several people saw him walk by, and some shook their heads. He knew the gesture meant disapproval, but he didn't know what he did to cause that disapproval.

Apollo walked for about twenty minutes before coming upon a small park with a boat launch and a small pier. He was getting hot, so he found a shady area between two bushes and lay down to rest.

***

Ryan walked into Ethan's bedroom and found him sitting on his bed playing a video game on his phone. "Ethan! Don't you ever get tired of that thing? You can't spend your life cooped up in your bedroom playing video games. You need to go outside and do the things twelve-year-old boys are supposed to do."

"I'm already doing what twelve-year-old boys do, Dad."

"If that's true, then our world is in a lot of trouble," Ryan said. "Why don't you go fishing? There's a park with a pier just down the road. You still like to fish, don't you?"

"I think I've outgrown fishing, Dad."

"You can't outgrow fishing," Ryan said, taking Ethan's phone from his hand. "Now go! This is not a request."

"What if I get into trouble? How will I call you?"

"I didn't have a phone when I was your age, but I survived. Now go!"

"Fine!" Ethan said, annoyed. He opened his closet, removed his fishing pole and tackle box, and headed out the door.

The pier was less than a block from the house. When Ethan arrived, there were no people around. He opened his tackle box, removed a lure, and attached it to his line. He cast it into the water and slowly reeled it in.

After several unsuccessful attempts, three boys showed up. One was about thirteen years old with medium-length sandy blonde hair. He was quite a bit bigger than Ethan, both in height and girth. The other two boys had short brown hair like Ethan and were about his size and age. The big boy spoke up and said, "Well, well, well. It looks like we have us an innerloper."

"I think you mean interloper," Ethan said.

"Whatever," the boy said. "This is our fishing pier. You don't belong here."

"Really?" Ethan said. "I looked around for your name but didn't see it anywhere. Do you have the deed?"

"The what?"

"The deed. You know, the paper that says you own this."

"We don't have no deed. What are you talking about? This is our pier, and you are fishin' on it. That means you owe us rent. I'm in a generous mood. I think twenty dollars should cover it."

"Sorry, but I left my wallet in my suit jacket."

The big kid grabbed Ethan's collar with both hands and said, "So you think you're funny, huh? How funny do you think it will be when I throw you in the water?"

14

Just then, the sound of a loud growl broke the tension. Everyone looked and saw a Doberman at the end of the pier, baring his teeth. He barked three times and then raced down the pier toward the boys. Everyone but Ethan jumped over the side to avoid the attack. Ethan was about to follow the boys into the water, but in his haste, his shoe got caught on one of the boards, and he fell. He quickly turned to defend himself against the attacking dog, but when the dog reached him, it sat down and raised its right paw high in the air.

Ethan looked astonished. "Are you giving me a high-five?" he asked before slapping his hand against the dog's paw. He then stood up, leaned over the railing, and called out to the boys, "Hey, you're right. Going into the water is pretty funny."

Ethan saw a tag on the dog's collar. "Apollo. That's a great name."

Apollo barked.

Ethan reeled in his line, closed his tackle box, and said, "Are you hungry?"

Apollo barked again.

"Okay, Apollo. Let's see if we can get you something to eat."

As they walked off the pier, Ethan said to the boys, who were now soaking wet on the shore, "You can have the pier now, and I won't even charge you rent."

They walked back to Ethan's house. When they went inside, Ethan said, "Dad, I'm home. I've got something to show you."

Ryan walked out of the kitchen, a towel in his hand. He saw Apollo and said, "A dog. Why is there a dog in our house? Whose dog is it?"

"His name is Apollo. I don't know where he came from, but he saved me from a group of bullies."

Ryan knelt down, petted Apollo, and said, "Good boy." He then checked his tag. He saw "Apollo" printed on the front and "CJL" on the back. "This tag is awfully vague. Who doesn't put contact information on a dog tag?"

"I don't know, Dad."

"Well, he can stay with us tonight, but whoever this 'CJL' person is, they will be looking for him, so don't get too attached."

"Maybe not," Ethan said. "Maybe he was dumped."

"Nobody dumps a beautiful dog like this," Ryan said.

"Maybe he ran away," Ethan suggested.

Apollo barked.

"You ran away?" Ethan asked Apollo, and he barked again.

"I think he is telling us he ran away," Ethan said.

"No, that can't be. He's a dog. He can't understand us."

"Apollo, do you understand what I'm saying?" Ethan asked.

Apollo barked again.

Ryan scratched his head and said, "Apollo, are you hungry?"

Bark.

"Are you thirsty?"

Bark.

"Are you happy?"

Silence.

"Do you want to go home?"

Silence.

"I hate to admit it, but maybe I'm wrong. Maybe Apollo is to dogs what Einstein was to people."

"Maybe his brain is like his superpower," Ethan said.

"Whatever he is, he's thirsty. Get a bowl out of the cabinet and put some water down for him."

Ethan got a bowl, filled it with water from the sink, and set it on the floor in the kitchen. Apollo eagerly lapped it up while Ryan fished several pieces of beef from the crockpot and put them on a plate. He put the plate in the freezer for thirty seconds to cool it a little before placing it next to the water bowl. Apollo made short work of the beef, licked the plate clean, and then looked up as if asking for more.

"I think he's still hungry, Dad."

"I can see that, but I didn't plan on three for dinner."

"What about the bones?" Ethan asked. "Dogs can eat raw meat, you know."

"That's a good idea," Ryan said. After he had cut the beef into cubes, he put the bones and the trimmed fat in a grocery bag and put that in the trash. He retrieved the bag and put the bones and fat on Apollo's plate, where he happily went to work on the former trash.

As Apollo worked on the bones, Ryan and Ethan sat at the table and ate the beef stew. "Tomorrow, we need to bring Apollo to the vet," Ryan said. "Maybe he has a microchip, and we can find out who he belongs to."

"If he ran away, maybe someone abused him," Ethan said. "Do we really want to return him to someone who would abuse an animal?"

"We don't know that he was abused. He doesn't look abused. Maybe there was a fire or a home invasion. Maybe something scared him."

"Does Apollo look like he would be scared of anyone?" Ethan asked. "I told you he chased off three bullies. He wasn't the least bit scared."

"Even so, the ethical thing to do would be to try to find his rightful guardian."

After they finished dinner and washed the dishes, Ryan found a travel bag with a long strap. He unhooked it and hooked one end onto Apollo's collar. "This will have to do for a leash," he said. "Take him for a walk, but stay close to home."

"Okay," Ethan said, and they walked out the door. Ethan took Apollo to the vacant lot next door. The sun had just set, and Ethan looked in amazement at the beautiful sky. He appreciated the beauty of nature, but that was not something he would admit to his father.

"Look at the sky, Apollo. Isn't it beautiful?"

Apollo looked up at the sky and barked.

"I knew you would agree."

After Apollo did his business, they didn't return inside immediately. Ethan sat on the bottom step, put his hand on Apollo's shoulder, and said, "I know it sounds selfish, but I hope we don't find your family. I want you to stay with me."

Apollo licked Ethan's face and barked.

"Sounds like you agree with me," Ethan said.

Chapter 4

Ryan woke with the sun the next morning. He brushed his teeth, showered, and dressed. When he was ready, he opened Ethan's door to see if he was awake. He saw him sleeping with his arm around Apollo. Apollo heard the door and opened his eyes, but didn't move. Ryan waved to Apollo and closed the door. He then felt silly for waving to a dog. Sure, Apollo was smart, but could he understand the subtle things humans do to communicate?

Ryan made coffee and started cooking breakfast. A few minutes later, Ethan and Apollo came into the kitchen. "Apollo smelled the bacon," Ethan said.

"I cooked enough for all of us," Ryan said. "We need to pick up some dog food later. He's a big dog, and I can't afford to feed him bacon three times a day."

Ryan put bacon and eggs on three plates and set them on the table. He then put one of the plates on the floor for Apollo. "Be careful, Apollo. It's a little hot."

Apollo picked up a piece of bacon and then dropped it. He smelled it briefly, then looked up at Ryan and whined."

"I told you it was hot," Ryan said. He picked up Apollo's plate and put it in the freezer. After a short time, he removed the plate and returned it to Apollo, who picked up a piece of bacon and practically swallowed it whole. He looked up at Ryan and barked.

"That means he likes it, Dad," Ethan said.

"Yeah. I figured that."

"We need to bring him to the vet today and have him checked out," Ryan said. "They should be able to scan him for a microchip."

"What if he doesn't have a microchip?" Ethan asked.

"We'll cross that bridge when we come to it."

After they finished breakfast and washed the dishes, Ryan looked up nearby veterinarians. He found one on the island and called the number. The woman who answered told him to bring the dog in as soon as possible. Ryan told Ethan to get the leash, and they headed out the door.

They pulled into the Pelican Point Veterinary Clinic five minutes later. Once inside, Ryan noticed the woman behind the desk was his next-door neighbor. She was dressed professionally this time, and her hair was brushed and tied behind her head.

"You're my neighbor," Ryan said. "'Brooke,' if I remember right."

"You have a good memory," she said.

"Not really. I remember you had an Irish last name, but I don't remember it."

"McCabe," she said, pointing to her name tag that read, "Brooke McCabe D.V.M."

"Oh, of course," Ryan said, embarrassed.

"Your name is 'Ryan Clark.' Did I get that right?"

"I'm impressed," Ryan said. "Your memory is better than mine."

"I'm only good at remembering names," Brooke said. "It's more like a trick. Whenever I meet someone new, I try to associate their name with some physical feature about them. I thought you looked like Ryan Reynolds, so the first name was easy."

"I'll take that as a compliment. What about my last name?" Ryan asked.

"I just thought of you as Clark Kent."

"Superman?"

"No, not Superman. Clark Kent. You seemed mild-mannered."

"I hope that's a good thing," Ryan said.

"I think it is. Now, let's take a look at your dog."

She led them to one of the exam rooms. Once there, she checked Apollo's eyes and then his ears. She looked inside his mouth. She listened to his heart, then placed her hands around his stomach and felt in several places. Finally, she said, "It looks like Apollo here is in great shape. I would guess he is not quite a year old, maybe eleven months."

"We need to find his owner," Ryan said.

Brooke looked at his name tag. She flipped it over and saw the initials. "That's weird," she said. "Why wouldn't someone put contact information on a name tag? I wonder whose initials are 'CJL?'"

"I don't know," Ryan said. "Can you think of anyone on this island with those initials?"

Brooke thought briefly and said, "No one comes to mind at the moment."

"What about a microchip? Does he have one?"

Brooke opened a drawer and took out a scanning device. She scanned the back of Apollo's neck several times with no results. She then tried different locations around his back and shoulders. Eventually, she said, "I'm afraid he doesn't have a microchip."

"What do you think we should do now?" Ryan asked.

Ethan spoke up. "I think we should keep him. Whoever had him before didn't care enough to get him microchipped or even put their phone number on his tag."

"It's not up to us to pass judgment on people," Ryan said. "Perhaps they just thought he would never get lost."

"He's not lost, Dad. He's the smartest dog I've ever seen. I'm certain he could find his way back if he wanted to."

"In what way is he smart?" Brooke asked.

"He seems to understand what people are saying," Ryan said.

"Really? Do you mean like in plain English?"

"Yes. At least at a basic level. He's truly amazing."

"Dogs can learn certain words, but they can't understand speech. He's probably just well-trained."

"I don't think so. I think he's intelligent. Very intelligent."

"I have seen a lot of well-trained dogs, and they really are amazing. Some seem very intelligent but can't understand spoken English apart from a few words."

"If you say so," Ryan said.

Brooke studied his face momentarily and said, "Okay, I can keep an open mind. Let's test him."

"What are you going to do?" Ethan asked.

"I will tell him to do something without moving my arms or shifting my gaze. Dogs can pick up on those subtle clues. That could be what he's doing." She folded her hands, looked up at the ceiling, and said, "Apollo, turn around."

Apollo turned around and faced Ethan, who had been standing behind him.

"Turn around again and sit down."

Apollo turned to face Brooke and sat down.

"That is impressive," she said, "but other dogs can do that too."

"Make it harder for him," Ryan said.

"Okay," Broke said. "Apollo, Bark."

Apollo barked.

"Bark two times."

Apollo barked two times.

"Apollo, Bark five times."

Apollo barked five times.

Brooke looked stunned. "Wow! That is completely unbelievable. Your dog can count."

"Have you ever seen a dog who could count before?" Ryan asked.

"No, I haven't. I heard of a horse that could count, but he was picking up subtle clues from his owner and the people watching. When the horse got to the correct number, the look on people's faces would indicate to the horse that he should stop."

"Do you think that's what Apollo is doing?" Ryan asked.

"I don't know. Let's find out. Everyone turn around so Apollo can't see your faces."

When everyone was facing away from Apollo, Brooke said, "Apollo, bark four times."

Apollo barked four times.

They all turned and faced Apollo again. "I'm impressed," Brooke said. "Let's try something else." She knelt and held both hands in front of her. She extended three fingers on her left hand and four fingers on her right hand. "Apollo, which hand has two fingers showing?"

Apollo clearly did not know what to do and gave a low whine.

"That's not fair," Ethan said.

"Oh, but it is. It shows he's not guessing. Let's try again. Apollo, which hand has four fingers showing?"

Apollo picked up his paw and pressed it against Brooke's right hand.

"That's right," she said and hugged Apollo. "He is not just smart; he's on another level. He might be smarter than a chimpanzee."

"How is this even possible?" Ryan asked.

"I don't know. He's either a freak of nature or a product of science."

"Science? Do you think someone created him? Like, maybe they genetically modified a Doberman to be super intelligent?"

"That is certainly a possibility."

"I know they are genetically engineering our crops, but I didn't know they were doing that with pets," Ryan said.

"Oh, yes. If you've ever seen those neon-colored fish at the pet store, you would know that kind of thing is already happening."

"If Apollo escaped from a lab, someone is surely looking for him. What do you think we should do?" Ryan asked.

"That is an ethical dilemma. You can't make an informed decision without knowing why he escaped."

"Apollo, do you know what a lab is?" Ryan asked.

Apollo just looked at him.

"Maybe he was never taught that word," Brooke said. "Let's try this. Apollo, were there other dogs where you came from?"

Apollo barked.

"Were there more than five dogs there?"

Apollo barked again.

"Were all the dogs kept alone in cages?"

Apollo hesitated like he didn't understand the question, but then he barked.

"He hesitated on that last one," Ryan said.

"I would guess he didn't understand a word but was able to guess based on the rest of the question," Brooke said. "Maybe he didn't know what a cage was called, but figured out what I was talking about from the rest of the sentence."

"That is very logical. I'm not sure if I'm more impressed by you or the dog."

Ethan looked up at his dad, surprised.

"Thank you," Brooke said, "but I would definitely be more impressed with Apollo. Understanding language is already extremely difficult for even the smartest animal, but filling in a missing word based on context is mind-blowing, especially considering his age. Imagine posing questions like that to your son when he was eleven months old."

"Wow! I hadn't thought of it that way. So Apollo could potentially become much smarter than he is now."

"No, not smarter, but more knowledgeable."

"Of course. Maybe he'll one day teach physics at MIT."

Everyone laughed, and Brooke said, "That would be something to see. In any case, I think we can be pretty sure he came from a lab somewhere."

"Either way, I think we still have to report him found. How does one go about reporting a found dog?" Ryan asked.

"Listen, Dad," Ethan said. "If we keep this quiet, nobody will ever find him. He can happily live out his life with us."

"He's not ours to keep, Ethan. We talked about this. We don't know where he came from or why he ran away. A dog as smart as Apollo is almost certainly destined to become some kind of service dog. If we keep him, someone desperately needing help won't get it."

"Your father has a good point," Brooke said. "Apollo would make a perfect service dog."

"I guess," Ethan said.

"Well, come up to the front counter, and we can talk about what you can do," Brooke said.

They followed Brooke out of the exam room and to the lobby. She walked around behind the counter, opened several drawers, closed them, and shuffled through several piles of papers on the desk. "Oh, here it is," she said and handed Ryan a sheet of paper. "A client made it for me. It's a list of ways to advertise a lost dog, but it also works for found dogs."

Ryan looked at the paper. It showed the top three websites for lost pets. It also suggested contacting animal control as well as local animal shelters.

Brooke wrote out the bill and handed it to Ryan. He looked at it and asked, "Don't you use computers for your billing?"

"Sort of," she said. "We have an entire vet management software package, but I would have an easier time flying the space shuttle. I'm not what you would call computer savvy. I have a part-time vet tech who is also my assistant. She will transfer this to the computer when she gets in."

"I'm surprised you don't have a full-time assistant. How do you handle unruly animals?"

"It's a small market here on the island. Sometimes, it's a stretch to afford the assistant I have."

"Really? Why did you start a practice here then?"

"I always loved this island. I grew up on the mainland, about ten miles from here. My dad loved to fish and would bring my brother and me here to fish about twice a month. He liked it because the island has no beaches, so all the tourists go elsewhere. Anyway, after veterinary school, I worked at a practice on the mainland for a couple of years. I saved some money, bought the house, and opened my practice here. It will be two years in September."

The door opened, and an older woman entered with a cat in a carrier. She sat down and placed the carrier on the chair next to her. Apollo appeared fascinated by the cat. He tried to get closer for a better look, but Ethan held him back, "No, Apollo," he said. "Sit down."

Apollo sat, looked up at Ethan, and then back at the cat.

"It looks like you have another patient. We should go. Perhaps you might want to join us for dinner if you're not busy after work?"

Brooke smiled and said, "I would like that."

Ryan and Ethan walked out with Apollo, who kept his eyes on the cat until they got outside.

"Good morning, Mrs. Harris," Brooke said after they left.

"Good morning, Dr. McCabe. I see that handsome man asked you out on a date. I'm happy for you. How long has it been? Two years?"

"Two years, three months, and nine days, but who's counting? Besides, it's not a date. He's my new next-door neighbor."

"Call it what you will, but I'm still happy for you. Two years is way too long. You need to get back on that horse."

"The last time that horse threw me and then stomped on me when I was on the ground."

"Sometimes you need to have a bad relationship to know what a good one feels like. Look at me. Frank and I have been happily married for thirty-five years, and it's my first husband I can thank for that. If not for him, I probably wouldn't appreciate what a good man Frank is."

"I suppose you have a point," Brooke said.

***

Apollo jumped into the back seat, and Ethan slid in beside him, buckled his seatbelt, and said, "It looks like you really like our new neighbor."

"She's okay," Ryan said.

26

"Just okay? I saw the way you were looking at her."

"What do you know about it? You're only twelve."

"I'm almost thirteen, Dad. Besides, I'm pretty sure you were my age once. Don't you remember?"

Ryan thought about Regina Schmid in the seventh grade and said, "Okay, you win. I like her."

Ethan smiled and put his head against the headrest. "Just so you know, I won't stand in your way if you want to date her."

"That's very generous of you, Ethan. It sounds like you like her, too."

"She's okay."

"Just okay?"

They both laughed as Ryan pulled into the parking lot of the island's general store. Surprisingly, they were able to pick up dog food, bowls, and even a leash.

After returning home and putting food in a bowl for Apollo, Ryan opened his laptop and visited the first website on Brooke's list. He filled out the information for a found pet until the option for uploading a photo came up. "Apollo, come here!" he called out.

A few seconds later, Apollo appeared before him. He looked at his tag, the name "Apollo" showing prominently in bold letters. "This won't do," he said and removed the collar. He then snapped a photo of Apollo before putting the collar back on. "Thank you. You can go back to whatever you were doing."

Apollo returned to Ethan's room. Ryan watched him go and shook his head in amazement. He knew Apollo could understand him, but it still seemed surreal. He hooked his phone to his laptop and downloaded the photo. He then uploaded it to the website. When finished, he continued to the next website on the list. He did not want to advertise Apollo's name. He knew Dobermans were valuable dogs and didn't want anyone pretending to be Apollo's owner so they could get a free dog. They needed to know his name before he would deal with them.

Chapter 5

Ryan pulled the lasagna out of the oven just as the doorbell rang. He removed his oven mitts and opened the door. Brooke was there wearing a dark red, skintight dress that came down to her knees. She had a bottle of white wine in her hand and handed it to Ryan. "I didn't know what you were cooking," she said.

"This is perfect, and so are you. I mean, you look great. I wish I had known you'd be dressing up. I could have worn something more fancy."

"I don't know. I think you look very handsome in that apron."

Ryan forgot he was wearing it, so he quickly took it off and invited Brooke inside. "Dinner was ready earlier than expected, so if you're hungry, we can eat now."

"I'm starving. Whatever you made smells delicious."

"We're having lasagna tonight," Ryan said.

Ryan had set the table and poured water before Brooke arrived. He opened the wine and poured two glasses. He then put lasagna on three plates and put them on the table. He opened a can of dog food, put it in a bowl, and set it on the floor near Ethan's chair. He then called to Ethan, "Dinner's ready!"

Ethan came to the table with Apollo by his side. Apollo lapped up the food in his bowl while Ethan sat down across from Brooke. "Hello again, Doctor, uh . . ."

"You can just call me Brooke."

"I'm glad you could make it for dinner, Brooke."

"Thank you, Ethan. I'm glad to be here."

She took a bite of her lasagna and said, "Wow! This is delicious."

"It was my wife's recipe," Ryan said.

"Your wife? You're married?"

"She died about two years ago."

"Oh, no. I'm so sorry. What happened?"

"If you must know, the answer is no, I am not seeing anyone now, and yes, I was once married. His name was John. I met him in college. We were so happy together. I thought he was the perfect man for me. Unfortunately, I wasn't the perfect woman for him. That honor belonged to Jackie, the woman who lived in the apartment below us."

"I'm so sorry," Ryan said.

"Don't be," she said. "Breaking up was the best thing that could have happened. I was young and naive. I convinced myself that I was happy. I told myself that the problems we were having were normal. They were problems that every couple had. If I had stayed with him, I would not be the happy person I am today."

"Well, I'm glad you're happy."

When everyone finished eating, Ryan asked, "What about dessert? Is anyone ready for cheesecake?"

"I am," Ethan said.

"Well, I really shouldn't," Brooke said, "but okay."

"That's the spirit, Ryan said and took the cheesecake out of the refrigerator. He put a small slice onto three plates and asked, "Is it okay if I give some to Apollo?"

Apollo was lying beside Ethan's feet when he heard his name and sat up.

Brooke looked at Apollo, smiled, and said, "I wouldn't make it a habit, but I think a sliver of a piece will be okay."

Ryan added cheesecake to four small plates. He gave Apollo's plate to Ethan, who placed it on the floor in front of him. Apollo sniffed it briefly and then gobbled it up.

"Did you like that, Apollo?" Ethan asked.

Apollo barked, and Ethan patted him on the head.

"I must admit, I will miss Apollo when he's gone," Ryan said.

"So, if nobody comes to claim him, can we keep him, Dad?" Ethan asked.

"That would be up to Apollo. If he wants to stay here, he can."

Apollo barked.

"Okay, but don't get your hopes up. Just because we haven't heard anything yet doesn't mean we won't."

When they finished dessert, Brook said, "Everything was delicious. Thank you for inviting me over tonight."

"It was my pleasure," Ryan said. "Are you leaving already?"

"I open early on Wednesdays and Fridays, so I should get some rest. The good news is I also get off early, so maybe we can hang out when I get home. I can show you around the island if you're up to it."

"Up to it? How could I say no to a private island tour by a lovely local?"

"Okay then," Brooke said as she got up. "I will see you tomorrow."

"I'll walk you out," Ryan said and followed her out the door. They reached the bottom of the stairs, and Ryan felt he wanted to kiss her goodnight, but wasn't sure if that would be pushing it. It had been two years since Amy died, and he thought it was time to move on. The decision was made for him when the door opened, and Ethan came out with Apollo. They trotted down the stairs and stopped next to Ryan and Brooke. "Apollo needs a walk," Ethan said.

"Well, I'd better go," Brooke said. "Goodnight, Ryan. I'll see you tomorrow after work."

"Oh, uh, yeah. Goodnight, Brooke."

As Brooke walked away, Ryan said to Ethan, "Please stay within sight of the house." He looked at Apollo and said, "Do you understand, Apollo?"

Apollo barked, and Ryan said, "Good. Don't let Ethan wander off."

Apollo barked again, and Ethan said, "Very funny, Dad."

Ryan went back inside, opened his laptop, and checked his email. He saw a message labeled "Apollo." Since he had told no one Apollo's name, he knew it must have been from Apollo's owner. He opened it and read, "Hello. My name is Dr. Kevin Miller. It is imperative that we meet to talk about Apollo. Please give me your name and address, and I will come to you. Other people may respond, but I ask that you please hear me out before you respond to any other inquiries."

He searched for "Dr. Kevin Miller" and found a lot of doctors with that name. He narrowed the search by adding "Florida" and then weeded through the results. On the second page, he found a LinkedIn profile that looked promising. He opened it and saw Dr. Kevin Miller listed as a geneticist who worked for Charles Jones Laboratories. So it was true. Apollo was developed in a lab. He looked up the company and saw it was about thirty miles from the island. That was a long walk for a dog. He must have hitched a ride from someone.

The tone of the email seemed strange. Ryan wondered if having Apollo in his house would be more trouble than it was worth. It was too late to change his mind, so he decided to see it through.

He wanted to call Brooke, but he realized he had never asked for her phone number. When Ethan came in with Apollo, Ryan told him he was going next door and would be back in five minutes. He walked over to Brooke's house and, on the way, noticed the sun had gone down, and the sky between the two houses was a beautiful mix of reds, oranges, and yellows. He knocked on the door and waited a long ninety seconds before it opened. Brooke was dressed similarly to the way she was when he first saw her. She was wearing pajama bottoms and an old T-shirt. This time, her hair was wet.

"She looked surprised to see him and said, "Ryan. Is everything okay?"

"I'm sorry," he said. "It looks like I caught you at a bad time."

"No, it's fine. What's up?"

"I got an email about Apollo, and I need a favor. I would have called, but I don't have your number."

Brooke turned to look inside her house, then looked at Ryan and said, "I'm sorry. I'd invite you in, but the place is a mess right now."

"You women always say that," Ryan said. "I'm sure it's fine."

"Okay," she said. "Come on in, but no judgments."

She stepped aside, and Ryan walked inside. He looked around and saw a disaster. Folded laundry lay on the dining room table. A large ginger cat slept on top of a pile of towels. Manila file folders and magazines were scattered about the coffee table. There were also several moving boxes piled along one of the walls in the living room and pictures leaning against the wall next to the sofa.

"I thought you said you lived here for almost two years," Ryan said.

"I have. I just haven't gotten around to unpacking. I've been busy."

"I guess you have."

"No judgments, remember?"

"I'm not judging you," Ryan said. "I'll be honest with you. The clean house you see next door is not me. My wife was always the clean, organized one. She always had to hound me about not making a mess. When she died, and I started working from home, I had no excuse. I needed to be a good example for Ethan. The truth is, if not for Ethan, I would have a hard time motivating myself to get organized."

"Listen, Ryan. I appreciate you trying to make me feel better, but it's not necessary. I know I'm not perfect. I know I'm unorganized and easily distracted. That will probably never change, and I accept that because I know I have plenty of good qualities that more than offset the bad."

"I don't doubt that," Ryan said, "but I didn't come over here to critique your home or anything else. I came to ask for your help."

"I'm happy to help you, Ryan. What can I do?"

"I got a strange email from a Dr. Miller. I looked him up. He's a geneticist at a place called Charles Jones Laboratories."

She thought for a moment and said, "CJL."

"That's right," Ryan said.

"So Apollo really is the result of some kind of genetic experiment."

"It would seem so, but he suggested others might contact me. He wants to talk to me before I talk to anyone else."

"Others? Why would there be others?"

"I don't know," Ryan said. "I've been turning it over in my head, and the only thing I can think of is that there is some kind of division within the company."

Brooke thought about it and said, "Hmm. If there is division, that probably means one side is good, and the other is bad. The question then is, to which side does this Dr. Miller belong?"

"Exactly. That's why I need your help. I don't want to give him my address. Do you mind if I arrange to meet him at your clinic?"

"I don't mind at all. I'm open from seven until three tomorrow. Why don't you tell him to be there at three o'clock? I'd like to hear what he has to say, too."

"Thanks so much," Ryan said and turned to leave. He turned back and said, "I got a lot of practice unpacking this week. I would be happy to help you with your boxes."

"Thanks, but I think I can handle it."

"Okay," Ryan said, "but you should know that I work cheap. A little food. Maybe a little wine. It'll be fun."

"That's a tempting offer. Maybe I'll take you up on it."

When Ryan returned home, he replied to the email with the vet clinic's address. He said he would be there at three. After he sent the email, he noticed another message had just arrived in his inbox. He opened it and saw it was from a man named Jack Strauss. He was inquiring about Apollo. He must have been from the other faction of the same company. He decided to ignore the email until he spoke with Dr. Miller.

Chapter 6

Charles Jones pushed the heavy metal door open and entered the lab. He held it open so the potential replacement for Dr. Miller could enter. "Here is where all the magic happens," he said.

Dr. Jessica Lopez was no stranger to laboratories. Twenty-five years earlier, upon receiving her Ph.D., she worked on the Human Genome Project until shortly after it was declared complete, even though the actual completion would happen almost two decades later. Since then, she has bounced from project to project, always getting resistance from within. In her mind, the scientific world was soft. Knowledge had taken a back seat to compassion. Nobody cared how people treated animals destined for food, but God help her if she treated one of her lab animals that way. She looked around and said, "Impressive."

Jones stopped when he reached Athena's cage. "This is one of our breakthrough dogs," he said. "The other one escaped, but we are working to find him and bring him back. Your job will be to reproduce Miller's results. These dogs will be pivotal in future military operations, so we need to eventually produce at least a dozen dogs per month, maybe double that number. You will also need to get this one to put on a show that will secure the military contract."

"What happened to Dr. Miller?" Lopez asked.

"He had a problem with putting these dogs into military service," Jones said. "How do you feel about that?"

"I can't think of anything more patriotic, Mr. Jones. I don't know Dr. Miller well, but I have seen him at a couple of seminars. I think he focuses more on the well-being of his lab animals than on the advancement of knowledge. You can't do proper research if you are worried about the animal's feelings."

"I think we are going to get along just fine," Jones said. "The job is yours if you want it. When can you start?"

"I came ready to work, Mr. Jones."

Just then, the door opened, and Jack Strauss came in. He said, "Mr. Jones, we have a lead on Apollo. Someone posted about a found dog. I sent an email last night, but so far, I've gotten no reply. I looked up the email address and found out who it belonged to. I then found an address for him in Tallahassee. I'm heading over there now.

"Okay, good. Keep me posted."

"Yes, sir. I will."

***

After breakfast, Ethan took Apollo outside for a walk. They came upon the pier and noticed that the three boys they had encountered the other day were there fishing. "Let's go say hi," he said to Apollo and walked to the edge of the pier. "Good morning. Have you guys caught anything yet?"

All three boys turned around. The leader pressed himself against the railing and said, "You keep that dog away from us."

"We don't want any trouble," Ethan said. "If you are nice, he won't hurt you."

"Are you sure about that?" the boy asked.

"Positive," Ethan said. "I'll show you." He bent down, whispered something in Apollo's ear, and then unhooked Apollo's leash.

Apollo slowly walked down the pier, and the boy said, "Are you crazy?"

"Relax," Ethan said. "He just wants to shake your hand."

When Apollo reached the boy, who was still pressed against the railing, he sat down and raised his right paw. The boy looked confused at first, but then reached down and shook Apollo's paw. Apollo then presented his paw to the other two boys, who also shook it.

Ethan rejoined Apollo near the boys, hooked his leash back on, and said, "My name is Ethan. This is Apollo." He held out his hand.

The older boy hesitated momentarily, then shook his hand and said, "I'm Bruce. This is Dillon, and that's Andy. They're brothers."

Ethan shook the younger boys' hands and said, "You look the same age. Are you twins?"

"Yes. Fraternal," Andy said.

"You must be new here," Dillon said. "Did you just move in?"

"A few days ago," Ethan said. He pointed down the street and said, "We live a few houses down that way."

Bruce pointed in the other direction and said, "We live a few houses that way. Andy and Dillon are my next-door neighbors."

"If you don't mind, maybe I can join you next time you go fishing," Ethan said.

"Sure," Bruce said. "Will you bring Apollo with you?"

"I'd like to, but Apollo isn't my dog. His owner may come looking for him soon."

Apollo whined and shook his head.

"Look at him," Dillon said. "I think he understood you."

"He did understand me," Ethan said. "Apollo is the smartest dog in the world."

"Everybody thinks that about their dog," Bruce said.

"I can prove it." Ethan put a hand on Apollo and asked, "Were you paying attention to the boys' names?"

Apollo barked.

"Good. Now show me who Andy is."

Apollo walked over to Andy and put his nose on Andy's hand, who petted him and said, "That's right. Good boy."

"Apollo," Ethan said, "how many people do you see?"

Apollo barked four times.

"That's incredible," Bruce said. "I've never seen a dog that can count."

"The vet thinks he might be smarter than a chimpanzee."

"No way," said Bruce.

"He might be part of some lab experiment," Ethan said.

Dillon said, "If he escaped from a lab, someone will definitely come looking for him."

"Yeah, I know. That's what I'm afraid of."

"If you want, we can hide him at our house," Andy offered.

"Yeah," Bruce said. "I'm sure my mom would be willing to take him in. He can sleep at a different house every night. That should confuse the people looking for him."

"I appreciate the offer," Ethan said, "but my dad would never allow that."

"Well, let us know if you change your mind," Bruce said.

"Thanks. I should probably get back home."

They said their goodbyes, and Ethan headed home with Apollo. When they arrived, Ryan said, "That was a long walk."

"I met some boys down by the pier."

"You did. Are they friendly?"

"They are now."

"That's great, Ethan. I knew this place would be good for you."

"Dad, I know a place where Apollo can go until everything blows over. We can just say he ran away."

"Ethan, you can't abandon your principles the first time you are presented with a challenge. You must always do what is right."

"I know what's right, Dad. Do you?" Ethan said before going into his bedroom with Apollo and shutting the door.

***

Jack Strauss arrived at the house he was looking for and parked on the street in front of it. The house looked quaint, perhaps two bedrooms, with an attached one-car garage. Jack guessed the whole neighborhood to be about forty years old. Maybe forty-five. He got out of the car and walked to the side of the house. He could see the backyard was fenced in with a four-foot chain link fence, but saw no sign that a dog was back there. Usually, a dog will wear out the grass around a fence, but Jack knew Apollo had not been with them long enough to do that.

He knocked on the door and waited. After thirty seconds, he knocked again. When no one answered, he peeked through the living room window. He saw dozens of boxes haphazardly stacked around the room. Just then, a van pulled into the driveway. Jack saw a man driving and a woman in the passenger seat. The man got out and walked around the van, putting himself between the woman and Jack Strauss. He was a large, burly man. He said, "What are you doing, peeking through my window?"

"I'm sorry," Jack said. "I knocked, but no one answered. I'm here about Apollo."

"Who?"

"Apollo. Aren't you Ryan Clark?"

"No. Ryan Clark was the previous owner. He moved out last week."

"Oh, I see," Jack said. "Do you have his current address?"

"No. I have no reason to keep in touch with the guy. I only know he moved to some island."

"An island? Where?"

"Near the coast, obviously."

"It's a big coast," Jack said.

"I guess you got your work cut out for you," the man said.

"Thank you for your time," Jack said before getting in his car and driving away. When he returned to the office, he reported what he had learned to Charles Jones and went to work to try to locate Ryan Clark.

Chapter 7

When it was almost time to meet with Dr. Miller, Ethan put Apollo into the car's back seat and climbed in next to him. Ryan got into the driver's seat, turned to look at Ethan, and said, "You don't want to sit up front?"

"I'm fine, Dad. Let's go."

Ryan smiled and said, "Okay."

They arrived at the vet's office about ten minutes early and went inside. There was a young woman behind the counter. She said, "Good afternoon. Can I help you?"

"Hi. I'm Ryan Clark. Dr. McCabe said it was okay to meet her here at three."

"She's with her last patient now, and I see nothing here about another appointment."

"It's not really an appointment. It's hard to explain. We'll just wait here."

Ryan and Ethan sat on chairs close to the reception desk. Apollo sat on the floor next to Ethan. The door to the back office opened, and a man came out with a large, brown and white Pit Bull. The dog saw Apollo and immediately started growling at him. Apollo stood up but did not attempt to escalate the situation. The man tightened his grip on the leash and said. "Max! Stop! Sit down."

Max sat down and watched Apollo while the man paid the bill. When they walked out, the man placed himself between Apollo and Max to avoid conflict. As they left, Brooke entered the waiting room and said, "Ryan. Ethan. How are you?"

"So far, so good," Ryan said.

The door opened, and a man walked inside. Apollo immediately went to him, put his paws on his chest, and licked his face.

"Apollo, it's good to see you, boy," he said.

Ryan stood, looked at Brooke, and said, "I guess we know what side he is on."

Dr. Miller held out his hand and said, "Hi. I'm Kevin Miller."

"It's good to meet you, Dr. Miller," Ryan said.

"Please, call me Kevin."

"Okay, Kevin. This is my son, Ethan, and this is Dr. Brooke Miller."

They all exchanged greetings, and Brooke said, "Let's go to one of the exam rooms. It's more private."

They all followed Brooke into the farthest exam room. She closed the door and said, "Okay, what's going on here?"

"Well," Kevin said, "as you have probably guessed by now, Apollo is a very special dog."

"Yes, we noticed," Ryan said. "You've genetically engineered him to be smart."

"That's right. My dream was to develop the perfect service dog: a dog who could understand almost any instruction and make decisions if its human was incapacitated. I believe Apollo and his sister, Athena, would make perfect service dogs. They have surpassed even my best expectations."

"Sister?" Brooke asked.

"Yes. My boss, Charles Jones, scheduled a demonstration with a potential client. Unknown to me at the time, the client was the Army. Jones wants to make war dogs out of Apollo, Athena, and all who come after. I'm not opposed to dogs in the Army, but that's not why I created them. Dogs like Apollo and Athena are much better suited to help people with physical and mental disabilities. So I walked out. From what I heard, Apollo and Athena escaped after I left. A feat even I thought was impossible. Athena was recaptured, but, as you know, Apollo made it all the way here. He must have gotten a ride from someone or stowed away in a vehicle."

Apollo barked.

"You stowed away in a vehicle?" Keven asked Apollo, who barked again.

He looked at Brooke and Ryan and said, "That's amazing. I never taught him what stow away means."

"He seems to be able to learn words through context," Brooke said.

Keven knelt and scratched Apollo behind the ears. "You never cease to amaze me, Apollo."

He stood up, and Ryan asked, "So, what do you suggest we do now?"

"I suggest you hide him. Maybe a relative that lives out of state can take him."

"No. You can't do that, Dad," Ethan said. "I told you I can hide him."

"You can't hide him, Ethan. I'm sure the people who will come looking for him will not be easy to fool."

Ryan looked at Kevin and asked, "Why don't you take him?"

"That won't work," he said. "Somebody from the company will surely check up on me."

"Another possibility would be to let Apollo go back," Brooke said. "You can instruct him not to cooperate with the Army. That way, they will have no choice but to stick with your original plan."

"It's too late for that," Kevin said. "Jones has already replaced me with a hard-nosed woman who cares nothing about the welfare of the animals. She only cares about results and will do whatever it takes to get what she wants. She has been all but ostracized from the scientific community. Jones hired her because she is just like him."

"How do you know all this?" Ryan asked.

"I have an informant on the inside."

"I feel like I'm stuck between a rock and a hard place," Ryan said. "I could get in trouble with the law if I refuse to return Apollo, but I don't want him to go back after what you told me about Jones and the new scientist."

"I'm not going to lie to you," Kevin said. "Jones will not wait for the law to intervene on his behalf. He will take back what is his."

"That settles it," Ryan said. "Apollo has to go back. I will not put Ethan in danger over this."

"No, Dad! You can't," Ethan said.

Apollo moved over to Ryan and pressed his nose on his hand. Ryan petted him and asked, "Are you telling me that you are willing to go back, Apollo?"

Apollo barked.

"I don't think you need to worry about Ethan," Kevin said. "Jones will assign Jack Strauss, his head of security, to retrieve Apollo. Jack is both tough and smart, but he is also a father and would never do anything that might harm a child."

"You're right. I got an email from Jack Strauss," Ryan said. "Well, if Apollo is willing to make a sacrifice to keep Ethan safe, I would also be willing to make a sacrifice for Apollo, as long as Ethan won't be in danger."

"Perhaps you can say that you gave Apollo to Dr. Miller," Brooke said. "That might confuse the issue long enough for us to devise a better plan."

"That may delay things for a couple of days," Kevin said. "I don't mind taking a little heat for a while."

"Okay, then it's settled," Ryan said. "When I get home, I'll email Mr. Strauss and tell him I gave Apollo to Dr. Miller. We then need to come up with a better plan by tomorrow because it won't take long before he figures out Kevin doesn't have Apollo."

"I told you, Dad, I know where Apollo can hide out," Ethan said.

"Where can Apollo hide out?" Ryan asked.

"He can stay with my new friends."

"I'm sure your new friends have parents who would disagree with that," Ryan said. He then remembered that he had moved Ethan to that island to try to get him out of his shell. Now that Ethan had made friends there, he felt he needed to help nurture that friendship. "On the other hand, your friends are worth considering, but only if their parents agree."

"Okay. I think we have the start of a plan," Kevin said. "We should all exchange numbers and keep in touch."

They all exchanged phone numbers and headed to the waiting area. When they got there, the room was empty. Brooke's assistant had already left for the day. After Kevin left, Ryan said, "Are you still up for showing me around the island? I'll buy dinner if you show me a good place to eat."

"That sounds like a good trade," Brooke said.

"Do you mind if I stay home?" Ethan asked.

"We'll be gone for a while. Are you sure you'll be okay?" Ryan asked.

"I'll be fine. Apollo will be with me."

Ryan squatted down, looked Apollo in the eyes, and asked, "Will you look after Ethan for me?"

Ryan noticed Apollo looked confused by the question and said, "Look after means protect or keep safe. Will you protect Ethan for me?"

Apollo barked, and Ryan said, "Thank you."

Apollo barked again.

***

Ryan drove home with Brooke following in her car. He let out Ethan and Apollo and said, "I'll be back in a couple of hours. Stay home and be good."

"Okay," Ethan said and closed the door.

Brooke Joined Ryan in the front seat and said, "Are you ready?"

"I sure am. Just tell me where to go."

"Do you like hamburgers?" Brooke asked.

"Who doesn't?"

Brooke told Ryan where to go, and they ended up at the island's southern end. The restaurant was in an old wooden building with weathered paint and a rusted tin roof. It stood beside a bustling marina and exuded a rustic charm. The smell of sizzling burgers mingled with the fresh sea air.

It was a takeout-only restaurant. Brooke and Ryan walked up to the window and ordered hamburgers and fries. Ryan paid, and the cashier handed him a pager. They sat at one of the picnic tables in front of the building and waited for their order. A pleasant breeze blew from the west.

"It sure is beautiful here," Ryan said.

"I agree. That's why I chose to live here."

"I wish Ethan could appreciate it."

"Give him time," Brooke said. "I don't know what he was like before, but he seems happy around Apollo."

"Yes, he is. I'm glad Apollo has helped him escape the rut he was in, but I also fear what will happen to him if we have to give him up. He may end up worse than what he was before meeting Apollo."

"I'm not a psychiatrist, but I think that is possible. Losing an animal can be devastating for some people. I hate to say it, but if you don't think you can keep Apollo, perhaps letting go sooner would be better than later. The more attached he becomes, the harder it will be for him to let go."

Ryan sighed and shook his head. "I just don't know what to do. This is quite a dilemma."

They talked for another few minutes until their pager started blinking. Ryan picked up the food and returned it to the table. He took a bite of the burger and said, "Mmmm. I see why you like this place."

"Best burgers in the county," Brooke said before taking a bite of her hamburger.

"So, do you think I should let the Charles Jones company take Apollo before Ethan becomes too attached?" Ryan asked.

"It's a dilemma, like you said. What does your heart tell you?" she asked as she picked up a couple of fries.

"My heart tells me to fight. Sending Apollo back feels wrong."

"I would fight too if I were you. Even if you fail, your son will respect you for trying," Brooke said.

"I hope that's enough."

When they finished eating, they took a walk through the marina. They came upon a houseboat with an older couple on the deck, sunning themselves. A small beagle lay nearby. When the dog saw them approach, he stood up and wagged his tail.

"Hi, Mary. Hi, John," Brooke said to the couple.

The older couple both sat up, and Mary said, "Oh, hi, Dr. Brooke. What brings you out here today?"

Brooke put a hand on Ryan's shoulder and said. "I'm showing my new neighbor around the island."

She introduced him, and they exchanged greetings. Then, the dog started barking.

"Oh, Bella. I didn't forget about you." Brooke moved close and petted the dog, who had her paws on the edge of the boat. She seemed to relish the attention.

How many dogs actually enjoy seeing their vet?" John asked.

"I have a feeling Bella enjoys seeing just about everybody," Brooke said.

"You got that right," Mary said.

After a few minutes, they said goodbye and continued walking. "Before I bought my house, I considered buying a houseboat to live on," Brooke said.

"Oh, yeah? Why did you change your mind?"

"I guess it just seemed like something retired people do. I'm still young. I wanted to leave my options open."

"Ryan considered what she might have meant by that. "Do you mean in case you want to start a family?"

"That's one possibility," she said without mentioning other possibilities.

Ryan didn't want to back her into a corner and decided to say nothing more about it. "I can see myself living on a boat after I retire."

"Unless you are a lot older than I think you are, we both have a long time before we need to start thinking about retirement."

"I'm thirty-two. How old do I look?"

"You look about that age. I thought you might be a little older because you have a twelve-year-old son."

I married my high school sweetheart right after we graduated. Ethan came along a little while later while I was in college. Those were difficult times, but I wouldn't trade being a father for the world."

"You seem like a good father."

"Thanks. So, how old are you, if you don't mind me asking?"

"I'll be the big three-oh at the end of December."

"Oh, you get to share a birthday with Jesus. I bet you loved that when you were a kid."

"Of course. What could be better than getting birthday presents with Santa Claus wrapping paper?"

Ryan laughed. "That would be hard to beat."

They got back in the car and drove around the island. Brooke pointed out each interesting thing that they passed. She even included a little gossip about some of the townspeople. When they returned to Ryan's house, Ethan was in the front yard with Apollo. He was throwing a tennis ball, and Apollo was catching it. They both got out of the car and watched for a minute. Ethan finally turned and said, "He never misses. He could play shortstop for the Rays."

"I think he would need to learn to throw for that position," Ryan said.

Ethan scratched his head. "I guess you're right. Maybe first base would be better."

"I would buy a ticket to see that," Ryan said.

Brooke pointed to the sky and asked, "Have you seen the sunset since moving here?"

"I have noticed it more than I did when we lived in Tallahassee."

"Judging by the clouds, I think it will be beautiful this evening. You should have a good view from your deck."

Ryan looked at the sky and said, "I think you're right. Would you care to join me for a sunset-watching party?"

"Well, I don't know about a party, but I think I can join you for a little while."

The raised deck went across the entire back of Ryan's house. Ryan opened the sliding glass door and revealed an empty deck except for two folding beach chairs and a small plastic table. "I haven't gotten around to buying outside furniture yet. Actually, that's not entirely true. Moving was expensive, and new furniture is not within my budget yet."

"No worries," Brooke said. "I went through the same thing when I moved here."

"Would you like a coffee or something?" Ryan asked.

"That would be great. I like cream but no sugar."

"Coming right up."

Ryan brewed the coffee, brought it to the deck, and sat in the chair beside Brooke. He set the two cups on the small table between them. The sky was starting to turn various shades of red and orange. "You're right. This is beautiful."

"Just wait ten minutes," Brooke said.

They talked and sipped their coffee for another ten minutes. By then, the sky was saturated with various warm colors.

"If God had an art gallery, this would surely be in it," Ryan said.

They talked until a few minutes after the sun went down, and then Brooke stood up. "I think I should be going. Thanks for a lovely evening, Ryan."

Ryan stood up and said, "I'll walk you out."

When Ryan opened the door, Ethan ran inside. "What's going on?" Ryan asked. "Where's Apollo?"

"We're playing hide and seek," Ethan called from the bedroom. "He's counting to ten. Don't tell him where I'm at."

Ryan shook his head. "Nobody will believe it."

They were about to walk out the door when Apollo ran inside. He stopped momentarily, sniffed the air a couple of times, then ran into Ethan's bedroom. They looked at each other and started laughing.

They walked outside and stood on the landing. "I had fun, but I should get going now," Brooke said. She kissed him on the cheek. "We should do this again sometime."

Ryan thought about the kiss as she descended the stairs. It was on the cheek. Was it a prelude for more to come, or did she just put him in the friend zone? "How about tomorrow evening?" Ryan called out as she reached the bottom of the stairs.

She turned and said, "Okay. I'll come by after work."

Ryan watched her until just before she entered her house. She turned to look, and Ryan waved before going back inside.

Ryan found Ethan and Apollo on the sofa. Ethan was eating a bag of popcorn while flipping through the channels. "I'm sorry," Ryan said. "I never made dinner for you."

"I'm twelve years old, Dad. I made myself a sandwich before you got home."

"I guess you're not my little boy anymore."

"Nope," he said as he popped a couple of pieces of popcorn into his mouth. He then gave the rest of the handful to Apollo.

"Did you also feed Apollo?" Ryan asked.

"Of course. I would never let Apollo go hungry."

Apollo licked Ethan's face.

"Don't give him too much popcorn. I don't think it's healthy."

"Okay, Dad."

Chapter 8

The next morning, after breakfast, as Ethan was getting ready to take Apollo for a walk, Ryan said, "Wait. I don't think it's safe for Apollo to be here any longer. Do you really think your friends will be able to watch him for a little while?"

"They said they would help. I guess it would be up to their parents."

"Let's ask them," Ryan said as he put his shoes on.

As they walked past the pier, Ethan said, "I'm not sure exactly where they live. I just know it's a few houses past the pier."

Apollo barked.

"Can you find them, Apollo? Do you remember what Bruce smells like?"

Apollo barked again.

"Okay. Find Bruce."

Apollo sniffed the ground as he walked while Ethan and Ryan followed. After two minutes, he walked up the sidewalk of a small, older house built at ground level. It was across the street from the water, probably constructed before modern hurricane codes.

Ryan knocked on the door. After thirty seconds, a girl around seventeen years old answered. She was tall and slender, with long, sandy-blond hair. She didn't look at them directly. Instead, she seemed to look past them, like something interesting was happening across the street. Ryan turned around but saw nothing, so he looked back at the girl.

"Can I help you?" she asked.

"Hi. Are your parents home?" Ryan asked.

"Just a minute," the girl said as she turned and walked back into the house.

A few moments later, a middle-aged woman came to the door. She was also tall and had the same sandy blond hair. "Can I help you?" she asked.

"Hi. I'm Ryan, and this is my son, Ethan. We recently moved into the neighborhood. My son just made friends with your son, Bruce. At least, I assume Bruce is your son."

"Yes. He's in his room playing with a couple of his friends. Do you want to see him?"

"No. We need to talk to you and your husband if he is available."

She looked inside the house before stepping outside and closing the door. "My name is Tracy," she said. "I'm afraid my husband died about three months ago."

"I'm so sorry," Ryan said. "Do you mind if I ask what happened?"

"It was a car accident," Tracy said. "Steve, my husband, was driving, and Ava was with him."

"I assume Ava is your daughter."

"Yes. They were checking out a college in Tallahassee. Ava is a talented pianist and wants to learn music in college. Bruce was sick that day, so I stayed home with him. Anyway, on the way home, someone in the middle lane decided he suddenly needed to exit. My husband must have been in his blind spot because he turned sharply into his lane and ran him off the road."

Ryan shook his head. "That's terrible."

"It was the worst day of my life. Fortunately, Ava survived, but she lost her sight. The doctors think she might eventually regain some of her vision, but it is very difficult for her now."

"It sounds like she has a long road ahead of her. Will she be going to college this fall?"

"That has all been put on hold until she learns to navigate her new reality."

"I wish her well. We actually came here to ask you a big favor, but it seems you already have too much on your plate."

"A favor? What kind of favor?"

Ryan hesitated but told her the entire story about Apollo. She looked at Apollo and then back at Ryan. "You mean this dog here is smart like a person?"

"He is very much like a person," Ryan said.

She thought for a moment and opened the door. "Bruce!" she yelled. "Come here! You have company!"

Ten seconds later, Bruce came outside with Dillon and Andy following. "Oh, hi, Ethan. Hi Apollo," Bruce said.

Apollo barked.

"You know this dog?" Tracy asked.

"Sure. Apollo is the smartest dog in the world."

Tracy shook her head. "Are you all putting me on?"

"No, Mom. He really is smart. Watch this." Bruce stood next to Apollo and said, "Okay, Apollo. Bark once for yes and twice for no. Do you understand?"

Apollo barked once.

"Do you want to go back to the lab where you came from?

Apollo barked twice.

"Do you want to stay here?"

Apollo barked once.

Tracy's mouth hung open in disbelief.

"Now, sit down and raise your left paw?"

Apollo sat and raised his left paw.

"Now raise your right paw."

He put his left paw down and raised his right paw.

Tracy was silent for several seconds and finally said, "I don't believe it."

"Are you here because you need to hide Apollo?" Bruce asked.

"Yes," Ethan said. "If it's okay with your mom."

"Can we, Mom?" Bruce pleaded. "It's just for a little while. He won't be a problem. I promise."

"After a long pause, Tracy finally said, "Okay, but just for a few days, and you need to take him for a walk several times a day."

"Yes!" Bruce said and high-fived Dillan and Andy.

Ryan lowered himself to one knee, put his arm around Apollo, and said, "You will stay here for a little while. Is that okay with you?"

Apollo barked once, and Ryan patted him on his side before standing up again.

"Thank you so much," Ryan said to Tracy. "Hopefully, I will figure out a way to keep custody of him before they figure out where he is."

"I hope you do, and I'm sure we'll be okay until then."

"Great. Thank you so much. I'll send Ethan back with Apollo's food."

***

When Ethan returned with Apollo's food, he found Bruce, Andy, and Dillon outside with him. Ava stood near the front door, listening. Apollo chased Andy across the yard. When he got close enough, he touched him with his nose. Bruce and Dillon yelled, "You're it."

Ethan laughed, "I can't believe you taught Apollo to play tag."

"He's good at it, too," Bruce said. "He's too quick for me."

They stopped playing and headed into the house. "That's quite a dog you have there," Ava said as Ethan walked by.

"Yes. He is very special."

Ava followed them inside and closed the door. She then carefully walked to the living room, found the piano, and sat down. She reached out and felt the keys on each end, then pulled her hands in and started playing.

The other boys had gone into Bruce's room, but Ethan stopped to listen to her play. Apollo stood by his side, also seeming to listen to the music. Tracy came out of the kitchen and said, "I'm making sandwiches for lunch, Ethan. Would you like to stay?"

"Yes, ma'am. I would like that."

"You can call me Tracy. We're not formal around here."

When Ava finished her song, Ethan clapped and said, "That was very good."

"Thank you," she said without turning around.

Apollo barked. This time, she turned around and said, "Thank you, Apollo."

"Lunch is ready! Come and get it!" Tracy shouted from the kitchen a couple of minutes later.

The boys piled out of Bruce's room and sat on the dining room table. Ethan hesitated, not sure if he should help Ava or not.

Ava stood up and walked toward the dining room. After two steps, she hit her leg on the edge of the coffee table. "Ow! Mom! Can we move this coffee table somewhere else? It's always in my way."

"That table has always been there. You know that," Tracy said. "If you want to go to college, you need to learn how to navigate your surroundings better."

"College? Are you kidding? I can't even leave the house."

"You can leave the house. You're just too busy feeling sorry for yourself to try."

"You really think that's why? Okay, fine. I'll leave the house. If I get hit by a car, don't be surprised."

She headed for the front door, and Tracy said, "Ava, stop."

Ava didn't stop. She walked out the door, forgetting to take her cane with her. When she got outside, Tracy called louder, "Ava!"

Ethan put his hand on Apollo's shoulder and said, "Apollo, keep her safe."

Apollo raced to catch up to Ava. He met up with her as she reached the street, which had no sidewalks. He brushed up against her so she would know he was there. She reached down and felt Apollo next to her. "Are you my babysitter?" she asked.

Apollo stayed silent.

"A babysitter is someone who takes care of small children."

Apollo barked twice.

"Okay, whatever. You can hang out with me if you want, but remember, I decide where we go."

Apollo barked once as they continued walking.

Everyone filed outside to see what was happening. "Apollo will watch her," Ethan said. "She'll be okay."

"I hope so," Tracy said. "Part of me wants to go after her, but I know this is exactly what she needs."

They all went inside and ate lunch. When they finished, all the boys met in Bruce's room. Ethan was fascinated by the racetrack that occupied a good portion of the bedroom. It was on a table that was about four feet by eight feet. A miniature town surrounded the track. It had houses, a bank, a gas station, a post office, and much more. "Wow!" Ethan said. "This is really cool."

"I've been adding to it since I was little," Bruce said. "My dad built the table for me when I was eight."

"I heard what happened to your dad, and I'm sorry," Ethan said. "I lost my mom a couple of years ago."

"Thanks," Bruce said. "I'm sorry to hear about your mom."

"Thanks."

"Have you ever raced slot cars?" Bruce asked.

"No. I've never met anyone with a track before."

Bruce looked at Andy and Dillon, "Do you guys want to go first?"

They both nodded, and Dillon said, "Sure." They placed their cars on the track, picked up the controllers, and started racing.

"We do ten laps, and the winner plays the next person," Bruce said. "The trick is to go as fast as you can, but if you go too fast around the turns, your car can fly off the track. If that happens, you can put it back on the track, but you lose that time."

Andy's car was in the lead going into the seventh lap, but he lost control around a corner, and his car almost flew into his lap. He quickly picked it up and put it back on the track, but Dillon had gained enough ground by then, let up on the throttle, and cruised to victory.

Andy gave his controller to Ethan and said, "Give it a try."

"Do a couple of laps by yourself to practice," Dillon said.

Andy put his car at the starting location and pressed the accelerator button. He did the first lap slowly and sped up on the second lap. His car flipped off the track at the first curve.

"Go fast on the straightaways and slower on the curves," Bruce said.

Andy made it around the track at a pretty good pace, but flipped the car halfway through the next lap.

"It gets easier with practice," Bruce said as he placed his car on the track.

They started racing. This time, Ethan made it all the way to the fifth lap before losing his car. He quickly put it back on the track and finished two laps behind Bruce. "Better luck next time," Bruce said.

They played for another half-hour until Tracy came into the bedroom. "Bruce, I'm going to look for Ava."

"Okay," Bruce said absently as he and Andy raced their cars around the track.

"I think you should give her more time," Ethan said. "Apollo's watching her."

"Has Apollo ever taken care of a blind person before?"

"I don't think so. Have you ever let Ava out of your sight since her accident?" Ethan asked. "I learned in school that birds learn to fly when their mother pushes them out of the nest."

Tracy stood there, dumbfounded. After several seconds, she said, "You are too young to be so wise."

***

Ava found herself outside and alone for the first time since losing her sight. She was scared but also angry. She was angry at her mother but also angry at the world. She would prove to her mother that she deserved all the sympathy that she sought from her. She would prove that being blind was a burden that mere effort couldn't overcome. When Apollo joined her, she was both relieved and somewhat upset because she suspected Apollo might keep her from getting the sympathy she so deserved.

Apollo walked alongside Ava on her left. If she drifted right, she would feel the grass under her feet and correct her stride. If she drifted left, Apollo was there to realign her. After walking for a short time, Apollo barked.

"What's wrong, Apollo? Is there another street here?"

Apollo barked.

"Is there a car coming?"

Apollo barked twice.

"I hope that means no. Okay, let's go."

They crossed the street, and Ava said, "We need to turn right on the next street. Do you understand, Apollo?"

Apollo barked.

"Okay, good."

When they reached the next street, Apollo barked.

"Are we at the next street?"

Apollo barked again.

Ava reached down and found Apollo's collar. She held onto it and said, "You lead the way."

Apollo slowly turned and led Ava onto a sidewalk. Once they straightened their pace, Ava walked on her own again. They crossed a small bridge and were soon on the mainland. "There's a restaurant ahead on the right," Ava said. They make food. I'm sure you will smell it when we get close. Find it for me, okay, Apollo?"

Apollo barked.

They walked for another three minutes when Apollo barked again.

"Are we here?"

Apollo barked.

Ava put her hand on Apollo's collar and said, "Okay, lead me to the front door."

They walked to the door of the restaurant and stopped. Ava felt for the door and pulled it open. "You can go inside," she said to Apollo, following him into the restaurant.

A middle-aged woman waiting tables stopped what she was doing and said, "Ava, how are you? I wasn't expecting you." She walked around the counter and hugged her.

"Hi, Aunt Margaret. I'm fine."

"Where's your mom?"

"She's at home. Apollo helped me get here."

Margaret looked down at Apollo and said, "Oh, my. He's a beautiful dog. I didn't know you were getting a service animal."

"Apollo is not our dog. We are just watching him for a while."

She patted Apollo on the head and said, "Let me get you two something to eat." She then helped Ava to a table. "I have an order to bring out, and then I will bring Apollo some water."

Two minutes later, she returned with a glass of water for Ava and a bowl of water for Apollo, which she set on the floor near him. He immediately started drinking. She looked at Ava and said, "What would you like to eat, Honey?"

"Can I get a hamburger with fries and another hamburger for Apollo without the bun?"

"Certainly. I'll have that up for you in no time."

A short time later, Margaret returned with two plates. She set the hamburger and fries on the table in front of Ava and said, "There you go, Honey." She then put the second plate, which contained a cut-up hamburger, in front of Apollo. "Bon appetit, Apollo."

Margaret sat across from Ava and asked, "So, what brings you here alone today?"

"I'm not alone. Apollo is with me," Ava said before biting into her hamburger.

"I see that, but I never see you without your mom. Don't get me wrong. I think it's great that you are getting out on your own, but I can't help but wonder what changed?"

"I just felt like visiting my favorite aunt," Ava said before taking another bite.

Margaret studied her face for a moment. "Really? Is that the only reason?"

Ava finished chewing and said, "Okay, fine. I was angry at Mom and needed to leave the house."

"What happened this time?"

"She thinks I'm feeling sorry for myself."

"Are you?"

"Well, yes, but that's not the point."

"What is the point?"

"The point is, I have a reason to feel sorry for myself. If Mom lost her sight, I guarantee she would be feeling sorry for herself right now."

"You might be right. If it happened to me, I would certainly not be happy."

"Can you tell her that?"

"It wouldn't make any difference," Margaret said. "Your mother is doing what a good mother should do. She is trying to improve the lives of her children. In your case, she feels that your attitude is making you unhappy, and she wants you to be happy."

"My attitude is not making me unhappy. My blindness is making me unhappy."

"There is nothing either good or bad, but thinking makes it so. William Shakespeare wrote that, and I believe it."

"Are you saying I can be happy by thinking about it?"

"Sure. Why not?"

"I don't know. That seems kind of far-fetched."

"Let's try something. I want you to smile."

"What?"

"You heard me. Smile."

Ava smiled for about a second and then returned to a somewhat depressed-looking demeanor.

"No! Not like that. I want you to really smile. Turn that frown upside down and hold it like that for ten seconds."

Ava smiled, and Margaret started counting, "One... two... three... four... five."

When she reached five, Ava started laughing. Margaret clapped and called out to the ten or so people in the restaurant, "Look, everybody! The blind girl is laughing."

Everyone clapped, and Ava said, "Stop. You're embarrassing me."

"Okay, but you have to admit that felt good."

"Okay, fine. It may have felt a little good."

"A little is a start. Look, Ava. I'm not saying it will be easy, but I think you can learn to be happy. You only have to want to be happy. So, do you? Do you want to be happy?"

Ava nodded and said, "Yes."

"Yes, what?"

"Yes. I want to be happy."

"Louder."

"I want to be happy!"

Margaret got up and hugged Ava. "It's up to you to make it happen. Now, I have some customers to take care of. I'll come back in a few minutes."

Margaret came back when Ava finished eating. She sat across from her and asked, "Are you okay getting home, or should I call your mom?"

"I'll be fine. Apollo will get me there."

"He must be one smart dog. Was he trained as a service dog?"

"No. At least, I don't think so. I didn't hear the entire story, but it seems Apollo escaped from a lab. He was part of some genetic experiment."

"Really? He looks like any other Doberman."

"I don't know about that, but he's incredibly smart."

"He sounds like he is exactly what you need right now."

"Yes. I think he is. It's too bad he will only be with us for a short time."

Margaret held Ava's hand and said, "I'm sure something will work out."

Ava stood up and said, "We should get going before Mom freaks out. Thanks for everything, Aunt Margaret."

"You're very welcome. Come back anytime."

They hugged, and Ava said, "C'mon, Apollo. Let's go home."

Chapter 9

Jack Strauss showed up outside Dr. Miller's condo a little after noon. The complex consisted of several two-story buildings, each with twelve units. Miller's unit was upstairs on the far left. Jack didn't drive the company jeep. He thought his personal vehicle would be less conspicuous. He backed into a guest spot across the street from the center of the building. He didn't want to show his hand by knocking on Miller's door, so he sat back and waited.

Before arriving, he had purchased lunch at a fast-food restaurant. He took a hamburger out of a bag and started eating it. He also bought French fries but left them in the bag, taking two out at a time to eat them. If Apollo were there, Miller would need to walk him. That's when he would act. He would confront Miller and take Apollo. If that didn't work, he had his tranquilizer gun and would use it on whoever gave him the most trouble.

Forty-five minutes later, Miller exited his condo, walked down the stairs, and got into his car. Jack waited until he drove away, then got out of the car. He slid the tranquilizer gun into his pants and covered it with his shirt. He walked up the stairs, and when he reached Miller's condo, he knocked on the door. Most dogs bark when someone knocks, but he didn't know what to expect from Apollo. He also thought there might be another person in the unit. He didn't want any surprises.

He waited thirty seconds and knocked again. When it was clear no one was home, he looked to his left and then to his right before taking out a set of lock picks from his pocket. He quickly unlocked the door and went inside.

He found himself in a short hallway. To the left was a doorway leading to a small kitchen. To the right was a wall with a large mirror hanging from it. Past the kitchen on the left was a dining area. Beyond that was the living room. To the right was a bathroom with a bedroom on each side of it. At the far end, a sliding glass door led to a screened-in balcony.

Jack looked around. The entire place was immaculate. He checked the kitchen. He saw a small water bowl and another small bowl half-filled with kibble. He looked in the pantry. There was no sign of dog food, but there were several cans of cat food and a small bag of dry cat food. He checked the bathroom next. There was a litter box under the sink.

The first bedroom was small. It had a double bed, a dresser, a nightstand, and not much else. The second bedroom was larger. It had a queen-size bed with a Siamese cat lying on it, propped up against a pillow. The cat watched Jack as he looked around for signs that a dog was there.

"Hi, Kitty," Jack said.

The cat responded with a hiss.

He checked the rest of the condo but found nothing that would indicate a dog had been there. Dr. Miller didn't have Apollo. Ryan Clark must still have him. He would have to pay him a visit.

***

Tracy absently washed dishes while she waited for Ava to return. She realized that she had been scrubbing the same plate for several minutes while she imagined all the bad things that could happen to a blind girl on her own. She rinsed the plate, and as she put it in the strainer, she heard the front door open. She turned the water off and raced out of the kitchen to see who it was.

Ava stood near the door with Apollo by her side. She kicked her shoes off as Tracy rushed to her side and hugged her. "I'm so glad you're okay."

"C'mon, Mom. Don't get all gushy. You don't have to worry about me. I'm almost eighteen years old. Besides, you're the one who told me to leave in the first place."

"I didn't tell you to leave. I said you could go outside."

"Which is what I did."

"So, where did you go?"

"I went to see Aunt Margaret."

"At the diner? That's over a mile from here, on the mainland. How did you get there?"

"Apollo guided me."

Tracy looked perplexed. Apollo guided you? How did Apollo know where to go?"

"I told him?"

"You told him? That's amazing. So you just gave him directions, and he followed them?"

"Something like that."

Tracy knelt and hugged Apollo. She pulled back and said, "You are very special, Apollo. Thank you for helping Ava today."

Apollo barked, and Tracy hugged him again before standing up.

Ethan came out into the living room after hearing Apollo bark. The other three boys followed him. "I told you Apollo would take care of her," he said.

"Yes. You were right," Tracy said. "Your dog is amazing."

"He's not my dog. He is here because he wants to be here."

"Well, I'm glad he wants to be here."

Ethan's phone beeped. He took it out of his pocket and checked the messages. It was a message from his dad telling him to come home and clean his room before dinner. "I have to go home," he said. He hugged Apollo and asked, "Are you sure you will be okay staying here?"

Apollo barked.

"Okay. I'll see you later, Buddy."

Ethan said goodbye to everyone before walking home.

When he reached his house, he noticed a car parked across the street, two houses down, but didn't notice the man sitting inside the vehicle.

***

"I'm glad you're home," Ryan said as Ethan entered the house. "You need to clean your room before Brooke gets here."

"Why? Will she be going into my room?"

"I don't know, but if she does, do you want her to think you're a slob?"

"She's your girlfriend. I don't care what she thinks."

"She's not my girlfriend. And you should care what people think."

"By people, you mean Brooke. You think that if my room is clean, she will think you're a good father."

"That's not the reason. Keeping your room clean is a good habit that will help you in life, and I want you to develop good habits."

"If you say so, Dad."

"Sometimes I feel like I'm talking to an adult."

"Well, I will be thirteen in a month."

"Oh, that explains it."

Ryan cooked dinner while Ethan cleaned his room. After a while, Ryan opened Ethan's door to check on him. He found Ethan sitting on his bed playing a game on his phone. His room was mostly clean, which was good enough. He wished Ethan would read a book or do something productive, but he knew nagging would probably backfire. "Dinner's almost ready. We'll eat as soon as Brooke gets here."

"Okay, Dad," Ethan said absently.

A few minutes later, there was a knock on the door. Ryan opened it and saw Brooke standing there with a surprised look. She had not gone home to change and was still wearing her scrubs. "I'm sorry. I didn't know this was a dressy occasion."

Ryan looked down at his tan slacks and white dress shirt and was glad he had decided not to wear a tie. "No, no, no. You're fine. All my casual clothes are in the wash."

Brooke smiled and said, "If I had a dollar for every time a man told me that."

They both laughed, and Ryan said, "Come on in. Dinner is almost ready."

"It smells good. What are you making?"

"Hot dogs."

Brooke looked surprised. "Seriously?"

"What's the matter? You don't like hot dogs?"

"I like hot dogs, but that's not what I smell."

"You're right. I'm making beef stroganoff."

Brooke took in the aroma and said, "It's too bad I'm a vegetarian."

Ryan looked shocked and said, "Oh, no! I didn't consider that. Wait, you had a hamburger with me."

Brooke laughed, "I'm just trying to keep you on your toes."

"Mission accomplished," Ryan said before motioning Brooke to the dining room table. "Have a seat." He then called Ethan to the table.

Ryan scooped the beef stroganoff onto three plates and carried them to the table. Before taking a bite, Brooke looked around and said, "I don't see Apollo. Did you find someone to watch him?"

"He's staying at my new friend Bruce's house," Ethan said.

Ryan nodded. "His mother was very nice about it. Her husband was killed in a car accident recently, and her daughter was blinded in the same accident. I felt bad burdening her with a dog to take care of."

"Oh, that's terrible," Brooke said.

"Apollo's not a burden, Dad. Ava, the blind girl, got mad at her mom and walked out. I asked Apollo to watch over her, and he did."

"That's great," Brooke said. "Dr. Miller said he was trying to develop the perfect service dog. It looks like he succeeded."

Brooke finally took a bite of her food and said, "Mmmm, this is delicious."

"I slow-cook the meat in a crock pot," Ryan said.

"You are going to spoil me, Ryan. How am I supposed to eat take-out after a meal like this?"

"You are certainly welcome to join us for dinner more often. Maybe I can teach you a few things."

"I don't know. Some people have the cooking gene, and some don't. I'm pretty sure the entire chromosome related to domestic work is missing in me."

"It's not missing. It's just mislabeled. We'll find it."

"Good luck with that," Brooke said before taking another bite.

When they finished dinner, Ethan returned to his room while Ryan and Brooke sat on the balcony and talked.

"Have you given any thought to Apollo's situation?" Brooke asked. "Do you have any idea what we can do to help him?"

"I like hearing the word 'we.' I'm happy you're willing to help."

"Hey, I'm an animal lover too, in case it wasn't obvious from my career choice."

"Of course, you are, but you're not just helping Apollo. You're helping me, too. I appreciate that."

"It's my pleasure to help. So, what about helping Apollo? Do you have any ideas?"

"I have the beginning of a couple of ideas."

"The beginning, huh? How close to the beginning are your ideas?"

"Just past the opening credits, but I'm working on it."

"I guess that's a start."

"If you want to help, maybe we can arrange another meeting with Dr. Miller. You said you have a short day tomorrow. Can we meet at three again?"

"As long as Dr. Miller is available, that works for me."

"I'll send him an email later."

Ethan came outside and asked, "Can I visit Apollo for a little while?"

"No, it's getting late. I also think you should stay away from there for a while, just in case someone is watching the house."

"You mean like that car that was parked across the street today?"

"What? You saw a car? Where?" Ryan asked.

"I'll show you," Ethan said, leading them outside and down the stairs. He pointed a little past Brooke's house and across the street. "There. It's gone now, but it was there when I got home."

"Do you know what kind of car it was?" Ryan asked.

"No. I wasn't paying attention."

"What color was it?"

"I think it was white."

"Does your neighbor have a white car?" Ryan asked Brooke.

"No, their car is red, but it wouldn't matter because they are in Maine for the summer."

"Okay," Ryan said. "We all need to be careful. If you see that car again, Ethan, let me know."

"Okay, I will."

"The sooner we can settle this Apollo problem, the better," Ryan said.

"I should probably get going," Brooke said. "I have to get up early."

"Okay. Make sure you lock your doors when you get inside."

She leaned in, kissed Ryan on the cheek, and said, "Thanks for worrying about me. See you tomorrow."

Ryan watched her walk home. He thought about the kiss on the cheek again. What did it mean? Did she want to keep him guessing?

Ryan went back inside, opened his laptop, and emailed Kevin Miller, asking for a meeting the following afternoon. He then closed the laptop and thought about his next move.

Chapter 10

After breakfast the next morning, Ethan asked, "Can I visit Apollo, Dad?"

"No. We talked about this," Ryan said. "If someone is watching us, you will lead them to Apollo. I'm sure you don't want that."

"No, I guess not. I just don't want Apollo to think I abandoned him."

"Apollo's a smart dog. He knows what's going on."

"What am I supposed to do today, then?"

"Today would be a perfect time to read a book."

"Aw, Dad."

"Don't 'aw Dad' me. I bought a book about Dobermans for your Kindle. Go read that."

Ethan's eyes brightened. "Really? Okay," he said before heading to his bedroom.

Ryan opened his address book, found the number he was looking for, and dialed. It was answered on the third ring. "Alex Palmer here. How can I help you?"

"Alex, it's Ryan."

"Ryan? Ryan Clark?"

"The one and only. How's it going?"

"It's going great. How are you? How long has it been? Two years now?"

"About that," Ryan said.

"I heard you moved to some tropical island."

"Not exactly tropical. We're just two hours from you. Maybe two and a half."

"So, how do you like it there?"

"I think it's perfect, but I have an issue here that I thought you might be able to help me with since you're the best custody attorney I know."

"Seriously? Your wife died. Why do you need a custody lawyer? Is it the in-laws?"

"No, no. Nothing like that. It's about a dog."

"A dog? Uh, you know I do family law, right?"

"I know a lot of people who consider their dog part of the family."

"Well, yeah, but legally speaking, it's different. I have little experience with pets. Occasionally, a couple will argue about who gets the dog, but, in my experience, it's always settled out of court."

"I just need some advice."

"Okay, tell me everything."

Ryan told Alex everything he knew about Apollo and mentioned how much better Ethan had been since meeting him. Alex listened, and when Ryan was done speaking, he said, "That is an amazing story. I'm sure this Charles Jones fellow can afford to hire the best attorneys money can buy. I think your only chance is to prove that the dogs are being mistreated at his lab."

"How can I do that?" Ryan asked.

"I'm afraid that is out of my wheelhouse, but I wish you luck."

"Okay, Alex. Thanks. You've given me something to think about."

Ryan hung up the phone and thought for a minute. He decided he needed to go shopping and searched for the nearest store that sold what he was looking for. He then went into Ethan's room and said, "I changed my mind. I have to leave for a couple of hours. If you want to visit Apollo, you can, as long as it is okay with them."

"I'm sure it will be fine, Dad. Let's go."

They got in the car, and Ryan backed most of the way out of the driveway before stopping to check the area. He saw nothing out of the ordinary, so he finished backing out and headed down the street, carefully checking his rearview mirrors.

When they arrived at Bruce's house, Ryan got out with Ethan, looked around, and then rang the doorbell. Tracy answered, and Ryan explained he needed to go to the mainland for a couple of hours and asked if she wouldn't mind if Ethan hung out with them for a while.

"Of course, Ethan is welcome," she said, opening the door wide so he could enter. "You should also know that Apollo is fitting in very well here."

"That's good to hear," Ryan said, "but we may need him back soon."

"Oh, did you find a way to keep him?"

"Let's just say I have the beginning of a plan."

"I hope you have the entire plan before acting on it."

"I hope so, too. Thanks so much for keeping an eye on Ethan. I'll pick him up when I return."

"You don't have to rush. He can stay as long as he wants."

"I have a meeting at three. How about I pick him up at two-forty-five?"

"That's fine. I'll let him know."

***

When Ryan picked up Ethan, he decided to bring Apollo along to the meeting. He knew it was risky but thought it was necessary. Considering Apollo's high intelligence, he thought Apollo should be involved with any planning that involved his fate. When they arrived at Brooke's vet clinic, Ryan retrieved a bag from the back seat, and they went inside. The office was empty, so they sat and waited.

After a few minutes, a woman came through the door holding a cat carrier. She was in her early fifties with dark but graying hair. Brooke followed her through the door. "Hello, Ryan. Hello, Ethan," she said. When she saw Apollo, her eyes brightened. "Hello, Apollo. I didn't expect you today."

Apollo barked, and Ryan said, "I thought he should be here."

"Aren't you worried someone will see you with him?"

"A little, but if we were having a meeting about your fate, wouldn't you want to be in on it?"

"I see your point," Brooke said.

The woman spoke up, saying, "So this is the great Apollo I've heard so much about." She petted Apollo's head and then scratched him behind the ears. Apollo leaned into the scratches as if he enjoyed them.

"This is Mrs. Hoffman," Brooke said. "She brought her cat in today, and I remembered she is a financial advisor, so I asked if she knew anything about Charles Jones Laboratories. It turns out she knows quite a bit and has agreed to help us."

"It's a pleasure to meet you, Mrs. Hoffman," Ryan said.

"Please, call me Mary," she said.

The door opened, and Kevin came in, followed by his former assistant, Jenny. "Hello," he said. "I hope you don't mind, but I brought along my former assistant, Jenny. She still works at the lab where Apollo came from."

Everyone said hello, and then Brooke introduced Mary to the new arrivals. Jenny knelt and hugged Apollo. He returned the affection by licking her face.

"I'm curious to hear what Mary has to say about the Charles Jones company," Ryan said.

"Tell them what you told me about the stock ownership," Brooke said.

"Well, Charles Jones started the company about fifteen years ago with the help of investors. The company went public about five years ago and invested heavily in genetic engineering with the money raised in the IPO."

"What is an IPO?" Jenny asked.

"It's an Initial Public Offering," Mary explained. "It sells shares of stock in the company. The initial shares are sold at a set price and then traded on the stock market, where the price can go up or down, depending on how well the company is doing. Does that make sense?"

"Yes, I understand," Jenny said.

"So, to get to the point, Charles Jones owns the most shares, but he doesn't own half. The last I heard, he owned less than twenty-five percent of his company. I bet a few board members working together could oust Jones as Chairman and CEO."

"How does this help us?" Ryan asked.

"Don't you see?" Brooke said. "If we can learn about the other board members, maybe we can make our case to them. Maybe they are animal lovers and would sympathize with our cause."

"I feel like you may be on to something," Ryan said, "but we need more. We must show them it would be in their best interest to part with Apollo."

"How could we do that?" Kevin asked.

"I have a few ideas," Ryan said.

"It's not enough to save Apollo," Kevin said. "We must also save Athena and the other dogs in the lab."

"How many other animals are there?" Brooke asked.

"Besides Athena, there are ten more dogs and a couple of dozen rodents and rabbits."

"I don't know," Ryan said. "Saving Apollo will be hard enough, but if all goes well, we might have a chance of getting new management in there. That will help the other animals."

"I can help," Jenny said. "I need the job to help pay for school, but I'm willing to give it up for a good cause. The new scientist they hired is cold-blooded. I don't think I will last much longer working for her, anyway."

Ryan opened the bag he brought in and took out several items. "I think I know exactly how you can help, Jenny."

After explaining his plan, he said, "There is one more part of the plan that I'm sure none of you will like. Apollo has to go back."

Apollo barked twice, and Ethan said, "No, Dad! That's crazy. Why would you send him back?"

Ryan knelt before Apollo and said, "This is your choice, Apollo. If it works, you, Athena, and maybe the other dogs will all be free. If it doesn't work, you all may be stuck there for a long time. It is risky. Do you understand what that means?"

Apollo barked.

"Good. Now, do you agree to go back to where you came from?"

Apollo was silent for several seconds before barking once.

Ryan patted Apollo's shoulder but said nothing. He stood up and said, "Okay, here's the plan."

They returned to Bruce's house, and Ryan explained to Tracy that he would be taking Apollo home. He told her the plan in a nutshell. She was disappointed but understood.

When they returned home, they saw a car parked on the street on the far side of Brooke's property. Brooke had returned home before them and was standing at the top of her stairs. A large tree in her front yard blocked her view of the car and vice versa, so she didn't hesitate to point in that direction when Ryan got out of his car.

He nodded and gave Brooke a thumbs-up. After going inside with Ethan, he said, "I'll take Apollo for a walk tonight."

"I want to go with you," Ethan said.

Apollo barked twice.

"It could be dangerous," Ryan said. "Apollo knows that. Stay here and wait."

"Ethan hugged Apollo and said, "I'm going to miss you, boy. Please, be careful."

Apollo barked and followed Ryan outside.

Ryan pretended not to notice the car and walked away from it toward the vacant lot. "If you have to go, now would be a good time," he told Apollo.

Apollo did his business, and they continued walking casually down the street. After a couple of minutes, a voice came from behind them. "I thought you gave Apollo to Dr. Miller."

Ryan turned around and saw who he assumed was Jack Strauss holding a tranquilizer gun. He wasn't pointing it at them, but it still seemed menacing. Apollo growled. "It didn't work out," Ryan said.

"Obviously. Now it's time for Apollo to come home."

"Apollo is home," Ryan said.

"Apollo is the property of Charles Jones Laboratories. If I have to, I will tranquilize him and carry him away. If you resist, I can always have the sheriff remove him for me."

"Apollo is here because your company is mistreating the animals in their care. Are you aware of that?"

"My job is to maintain security, not babysit lab animals. The more time I spend chasing after a dog, the less time I have to do my job. So, if you don't mind, hand over Apollo so I can get back to work."

Ryan sighed, "I will give you Apollo if you promise to look after him and ensure he is treated humanely."

"I have no influence in that area."

Ryan knelt and unhooked Apollo's leash but held on to his collar. "I'm going to tell Apollo to run and then block you from shooting him with your tranquilizer gun. That will delay you from getting back to your job for quite a while."

Jack hesitated and finally said, "Okay, you win. I promise I will do what I can to look after him."

Ryan clipped the leash back onto Apollo's collar and then hugged him. "Please go with this man, and don't give him trouble. We will try to get you out of there." He stood and handed the leash to Jack.

Apollo whined but reluctantly turned and walked with Jack back to his car.

When Ryan returned home, Ethan asked, "Did that man take Apollo?"

"Yes, he did."

"Did he suspect anything?"

"I don't think so. Apollo was a good actor."

***

Brooke watched from her window. She saw Jack returning to his car with Apollo. She then saw Ryan walking up the street. She went downstairs to meet him.

"That must have been hard to do," she said.

"It sure was. I'm going to miss having Apollo around here. He really helped Ethan. Now I'm worried Ethan will return to his old ways."

"It's not over yet. We all have something to work for now, including Ethan."

"You're probably right. It's good to have a goal. It just bothers me that the only way to improve Apollo's life is to make it worse first."

Brooke reached out and took Ryan's hand. "You're a compassionate man. I like that about you."

They looked each other in the eyes and then slowly leaned in to kiss. Before their lips touched, the door opened, and Ethan yelled, "Dad! When's dinner? I'm starving."

Ryan turned to Ethan and yelled, "Give me a minute."

When Ethan closed the door, Ryan turned back to Brooke and said, "I'm sorry. Would you like to join us for dinner? I didn't plan anything, but plenty of leftovers are in the fridge."

"I'd love to, but I have some things I have to do at home tonight. Can I take a rain check?" Brooke asked.

"Of course. Maybe tomorrow."

***

Jack didn't return with Apollo until well after six. Some departments had a night shift, but the place seemed empty in the evenings. He walked Apollo to the genetics lab, opened the door, and went inside. He was surprised to see that Dr. Lopez was there working late. She turned and saw Jack with a Doberman. "So this must be the elusive

Apollo," she said as she stood up from her chair. She took a couple of steps towards them, held out her hand, and said, "I'll take him."

Jack handed Dr. Lopez the leash. "I have a special surprise for you," she said, leading Apollo to a small crate barely big enough for him to turn around in.

"Get in there," she said.

Apollo didn't move.

"Apollo! Get in the crate!" she commanded.

Apollo looked at Jack and whined.

"Why put him in there?" Jack asked. "What's wrong with his normal pen?"

"He needs to learn that there are consequences to his actions. All my test subjects must be cooperative, or else they're no good to me."

"I understand, but you can catch more flies with honey than vinegar."

"I'm not interested in catching flies. Are you questioning my methods?"

"No, Ma'am, but I've had dogs before, and I'm merely pointing out that they are loyal to the ones they love."

"When you receive your degree in animal psychology, I would be happy to discuss this with you further; until then, have a good night, Mr. Strauss." She turned to Apollo and pushed him into the crate. He reluctantly obeyed.

Jack stood and watched Dr. Lopez for several seconds before leaving the lab.

Chapter 11

Jenny arrived at the lab early the following morning. One of her jobs was to walk all the dogs before starting her other duties. Normally, she would walk Apollo and Athena together, but since Apollo ran away, she had been walking Athena with another dog.

She looked at Apollo's empty cage and sighed. She then took Athena out of her pen and put a leash on her. She was about to open another pen when Athena pulled on the leash and practically dragged Jenny to the other side of the lab. When she reached Apollo's cage, they licked each other through the cage's bars.

Jenny, surprised, said, "Apollo! I don't believe it. You're back." She knelt and quickly opened the cage. Apollo sprang out, put both paws on Jenny's shoulders, and licked her face. She hugged him, backed away, and asked, "Who put you in that tiny cage? Was it Dr. Heartless?"

Apollo remained quiet.

It was a rhetorical question, but she decided she wanted Apollo to answer it, so she asked again in another way. "Did a woman make you go in that little cage?"

Apollo barked.

"I'm sorry you have to put up with her," Jenny said as she walked outside with the two dogs.

When she returned, she put Apollo and Athena in their pens and took out two German shepherds, Eros and Thea. As she prepared to bring them outside, Dr. Lopez arrived. "Good morning, Doctor," Jenny said in the most pleasant voice she could muster. "I didn't expect you to be here on a Saturday."

"Why not? Do you think I'm one of those nine-to-five kinds of people?"

"No, but..."

"Why in the world is Apollo in his pen?" Lopez asked, annoyed.

"That's where he belongs," Jenny said.

"No, no, no! He is being punished for escaping. You probably set us back an entire day with your thoughtlessness."

"Jenny's eyes widened in shock. "Thoughtlessness?"

Lopez ignored her, opened Apollo's pen, grabbed his collar, and attempted to pull him out, but he resisted, growling.

"Stop!" Jenny said. "You can't put him in that little cage. It's far too small. He can't even stand up in it."

Lopez turned to Jenny with a look of contempt. "You are here to learn, not to give advice. The first thing you need to learn is respect for those above you. There are plenty of interns who would pay to take your place."

Jenny wanted to tell her off, but she knew she needed to keep her cool for a little while longer. "Let me handle Apollo," she said.

"Thank you very much for doing your job," Lopez said before letting go of Apollo and walking away.

"Stay," Jenny said to Eros and Thea before walking to Apollo. She knelt in front of him, put her hand on his collar, and whispered, "I'm sorry. I know it's uncomfortable, but it's just for a little while longer. Okay?"

Apollo licked Jenny's face and allowed her to lead him to the small cage. He whined loud enough for Dr. Lopez to hear before getting inside. Jenny then brought Eros and Thea outside for their walk. When she finished walking all the dogs, Dr. Lopez told her to take Athena out for some tests.

"What about Apollo?" she asked.

"Apollo hasn't been punished long enough for escaping. Now, go on."

Jenny removed Athena from her pen and brought her to the small obstacle course set up inside the lab. Dr. Lopez got up from her chair, picked up a bucket of balls, and dumped them on the ground. She said, "Athena, bring me all the yellow balls."

Athena didn't move.

"Athena!" Lopez said sternly. "Bring me all the yellow balls."

"I think she's upset that her brother is in that little cage," Jenny said.

"Athena needs to learn that I run the show around here." Lopez walked over to Athena, knelt in front of her, and said, "Apollo will stay in that cage and get no food or water until you decide to do what you are told. Do you understand?"

Athena looked Lopez in the eyes. She didn't growl, but she showed her teeth.

"I have another cage just like that for you if you don't cooperate. You can both go without food or water if that's how you want to behave."

Lopez returned to where she was, and Jenny whispered to Athena, "Just do what she wants. We'll get you out of here soon. Hopefully."

"Let's try this again, Lopez said. "Athena, bring me all the yellow balls."

There were four yellow balls in the mix. After a moment's hesitation, Athena carried the yellow balls one at a time and dropped them at Lopez's feet. She then returned to Jenny and sat down.

"I think it's time to see if Apollo will cooperate with us now," Lopez said. "Bring him out."

Jenny took Apollo from his small cage and brought him next to Athena. He sat next to her as she licked his face."

"Apollo, bring me all the blue balls," Lopez said.

Apollo stared at Lopez but didn't move.

"Jenny, put Athena in Apollo's cage."

"What?" Jenny said incredulously.

"You heard me."

Apollo growled at Dr. Lopez, who said, "You will do what I say, or Athena will go in that cage."

Apollo sat for several seconds before bringing the blue balls to Dr. Lopez. He returned to Athena and sat down next to her.

"Now, was that so hard?" Lopez asked.

Apollo stared at Lopez but made no sound.

"I think they are ready for another demonstration. Put them back."

Jenny led them back to their pens, but Lopez stopped her. "No! Apollo goes back in there," she said, pointing to the small cage.

"What? Why? They did what you asked."

"Yes, they did, but I need to know they will continue to do what I ask. Apollo will stay in that cage until after a successful demonstration. When I say successful, I mean successful. They will not do what they did last time or else."

Lopez went to her desk, picked up the phone, and dialed a number. When it was answered, she said, "Mr. Jones, it's Dr. Lopez. We're ready for another demonstration."

Chapter 12

Brooke woke up earlier than usual for a Sunday, showered, and was in her bedroom putting on makeup when she heard the doorbell ring. She thought it might be Ryan, but she wasn't expecting him so early. She hadn't dressed yet and was still wearing her oversized T-shirt and pajama bottoms. Ryan had already seen her dressed like that, so she wasn't concerned about how she looked.

She opened the door and was surprised at who she saw. A man wearing an Army uniform and holding a dozen roses stood at her door. He was tall and handsome, in his late twenties, with short brown hair and a big smile.

"John! What are you doing here?" Brooke said as she stepped outside to hug him.

When she stepped back, John handed her the flowers.

"Oh, these are beautiful. Come on in," she said, backing away so he could step inside. "That was very nice of you, but don't you think it's a little weird bringing flowers to your sister?"

"Not at all. You deserve it. Unless something has changed, it's been a while since you had a man in your life, so I figured someone should bring you flowers."

"Well, actually, I did meet someone recently."

"You did? That's great. Who is he?"

"His name is Ryan. He moved in next door about a week ago. I like him, but it's not serious."

"Not now, but it could be, right?"

"I don't think so," Brooke said. "My life is fine the way it is. I don't need a man complicating it. I'd rather just be friends."

"Brooke, it's been two years. No, it's been over two years. You need to get over what happened and move on with your life."

"That's easy for you to say. You've never had your heart broken. I prefer not to go through that again."

"That's called failure. Everyone fails. It's Mother Nature's best teaching tool. If you want to succeed in anything, including relationships, you must fail first, sometimes multiple times. The only people who don't fail are people who don't try, and those people end up lonely and unhappy, which is the worst kind of failure."

"Okay, you win. I give up."

"So you will give this man a chance?"

"I will consider it," Brooke said.

Brooke carried the flowers to the kitchen, removed a vase from under the sink, and filled it with water. She put the roses in the vase, pushed a pile of mail aside, and set it on the dining room table. "These are really lovely," she said.

"It looks like you still need a cleaning person."

"I'm sure you didn't come here to judge me?"

"No, I didn't. I came because I got your message that you wanted to talk to me."

"I assumed you would call. You didn't have to come all the way out here."

"I had the weekend off, and I thought this would be a great time to see my older sister."

"Don't start with that older sister stuff again. We're twins. We're the same age."

"No. You were born eight minutes before I was."

"That's true, but we were conceived at the same time. That makes us the same age."

John smiled. "If you say so, Sis. So, what did you want to talk about?"

"Do you know a General Adams?"

"Yes, I know him. Why?"

"Do you think you can get a letter to him for me?"

"A letter? Why in the world would you want to write to General Adams?"

Brooke told him the entire story about Apollo and what they were planning to do. John looked at her in amazement. "Are you pulling my leg?"

"No, John. I'm serious. This is important to me."

"Okay, I'll give him your letter, but it might be easier if you emailed him. I can give you his email address."

"You know I'm no good at that computer stuff."

"How did you grow up in the twenty-first century without learning how to use a computer?"

"I can use a computer. I'm just not good at it," Brooke said as she looked through drawers in her china cabinet. "Plus, the only computer I own is at the clinic."

She found the folder she was looking for and removed a piece of paper before returning the folder to the drawer. She moved some magazines aside, set the paper on the coffee table, and started writing. When she finished, she opened another drawer, pulled out an envelope, folded the paper, and put it in the envelope. She wrote "General Adams" on it and handed it to her brother.

"It's been years since I've seen a handwritten letter," John said.

"That means it's more likely to get the General's attention."

"I suppose you're right about that."

"I hate to tell you, John, but I didn't expect you to come here, and I made plans with my neighbor this morning. I'm sure you could come along if you want."

"Oh, I wouldn't dream of it. I'm happy you have a chance at love, and I don't want to interfere with that."

"It's not like that. We're just going to talk to some people about Apollo."

"It's fine, Brooke. I didn't come here expecting you would drop your plans for me. I wanted to go out for a drive and see my sister. Now that I accomplished that, I'll just be heading back."

Brooke hugged John and said, "I'm sorry. The next time you have some time off, why don't you come and stay for a few days? I'll clean out the spare bedroom. I'm pretty sure there's a bed in there."

John laughed. "You haven't changed a bit in your old age."

Brooke playfully slapped John on the arm and said, "Apparently, you haven't changed either."

***

After breakfast, Ethan said he wanted to hang out with his new friends. Ryan liked his new friends because they were not addicted to their phones and did the kind of things he did when he was young, but he had plans for the day and didn't want to leave Ethan alone for so long.

"Sorry, Buddy, but Brooke and I are going to the mainland for a few hours, and I want you to come along."

"C'mon, Dad. I'm old enough to stay home alone. You know that."

"I'm okay with leaving you home for short trips into town, but I'll be gone too long, and we'll be too far away if anything happens to you."

"I'm sure Bruce's mom wouldn't mind if I hung out there for a few hours."

Ryan sighed. "Okay, fine. Go to Bruce's house and explain that I will be gone for a few hours, and ask if it's okay that you stay there."

When Ethan left, Ryan cleaned up the kitchen. He then finished getting ready. He had told Brooke to plan on going around nine-thirty. He looked at the clock, which read 9:15. It was close enough. He stepped out the door and was about to lock it when he saw a blue Ford Mustang pull into Brooke's driveway. An army officer got out carrying a bouquet of roses. Ryan watched him climb the steps and ring the doorbell. A few moments later, Brooke opened the door, hugged the man, and invited him inside.

Feeling dejected, Ryan went back inside and sat on the sofa. He put his head back, wondering what he had done wrong. Did Brooke really think of him as just a friend? He should have told her how he felt days ago. It was his fault for being so slow. He was introverted as a teenager but thought he had gotten over it. Apparently, he hadn't.

He was jarred back to reality when his phone rang. It was Ethan. "Hello, Ethan. Did you talk to Stacy?"

"Yes. She said it would be her pleasure to keep an eye on me."

"She used the word 'pleasure?'"

"That's exactly what she said. Do you think I would use a word like that?"

"No, I guess not. Okay, well, I want you to be on your best behavior. I'll pick you up this afternoon."

"Okay, Dad. Thanks."

A half-hour later, there was a knock at the door. Ryan got up to answer it and saw Brooke standing there. "Did you forget about me?" She asked.

What? No. I... uh... I thought you forgot about me."

"You were going to come by and get me, remember."

"I do remember, but when I saw you had a man at your house, I thought your plans had changed."

Brooke paused for a moment and smiled. "Oh, you must have seen John. Do you think I shouldn't have a man at my house?"

"No. You're free to have anyone you want in your house. I just thought you forgot about our plans."

Brooke's smile grew bigger. "You're jealous."

"Jealous? Me? No. I'm not jealous."

"If you say so."

"Okay, fine. I'm a little jealous. I like you, Brooke, and I thought we had chemistry. I should have told you sooner, but it's been so long since I've courted anyone that I guess I forgot how to act."

Brooke stepped in closer and put her hands on Ryan's arms. "You didn't forget how to act. You've been a perfect gentleman. It's my fault. After being hurt the last time, I'm just not ready to go through that pain again. I hope you understand."

"I guess I understand, but I'm not ready to give up on you yet."

"That is very sweet, Ryan, but I don't want to disappoint you."

"I don't want you to disappoint me."

"So then we agree."

"Yes. Wait, what?"

"Are we ready to go?" Brooke asked.

"No. I have one more question. If you don't want to get involved with anyone, who was that man at your house this morning?"

"That man was my brother, John."

"Your brother? That was your brother?"

"Yes. He had the weekend off and came to visit."

"Oh, I'm sorry. I wish I had known earlier. You didn't have to send him away. I would have been happy if he had joined us."

"I told him it would be okay, but he didn't want to be a third wheel."

"I'd be happy to meet him. If it's not too late, maybe you can call him and tell him to come back."

"I know you're trying to be nice, Ryan, but the truth is, I'm glad he's not coming. He's been pushing me to get into a relationship, and I don't want to think about that right now."

"I get it. Ethan said he would be okay with me dating you. He's not exactly pushing me, but he knows enough time has passed since his mom died."

"Speaking of Ethan, where is he?"

"He's spending the day with his friends. I told him I'd pick him up on the way home this afternoon. I want to know more about your brother. Is he older or younger than you?"

"He loves to tout the fact that he's younger than me, but it's only by eight minutes."

"Oh, so you two are twins. That's interesting because two of Ethan's new friends are also twins."

"I think that is much more common now because of fertility clinics."

"I hadn't considered that. Did your parents go to a fertility clinic?"

"No. John and I are natural anomalies."

"You are different, I'll give you that, but in a good way."

When they got in the car, Brooke asked, "Where are we going first?"

"We're going to see Jenny, Dr. Miller's assistant."

"You mean Kevin. He told us to call him Kevin."

"Yes, Kevin. That's right."

"So, why are we seeing her and not Kevin?"

"She emailed me and said she had what I asked her to get."

"Oh, really. I expected that it would take longer."

"Unfortunately for Apollo, it didn't."

"It feels like we need to act quickly on this," Brooke said.

Ryan nodded but said nothing. He put Jenny's address into his phone and clicked the directions button. A map appeared, and Ryan said, "She's just outside of Gainsville, a little over an hour from here."

"Where is the lab Apollo escaped from?" Brooke asked as they started driving.

"It's about thirty miles from here. We'll pass fairly close to it on the way."

"Do you think we should scope the place out in case we want to break Apollo out of there?"

"Good idea. Then we can buy a couple of ninja outfits and wait for a moonless night."

They both laughed, and Ryan said, "I already checked it out on my computer."

"Really? You can do that?"

"Sure. Didn't you ever use the street view on your phone?"

Brooke took her small flip phone out of her purse. She opened it and looked through the menu. "I don't think my phone has something like that," she said.

Ryan looked at her, shook his head, and said, "You're kidding me. That's what you use for a phone? I didn't know they still made those."

"Of course, they still make them. It's not that old. What's wrong with it?"

"Nothing's wrong with it. It's just... well... old-fashioned."

"It's a phone. It does phone stuff. That's all I need."

"Phone stuff?"

"You know what I mean. So, did you see anything interesting when you looked at the place?"

"I saw a tall fence surrounding it, and the only way in is through a gate controlled by a security guard."

Brooke looked at him momentarily and said, "You're not really thinking of breaking in, are you?"

"No. Of course not. Apollo will be breaking out."

"Tell me you have a plan."

"That depends on how you define 'plan.'"

They easily found Jenny's apartment complex. It looked less like an apartment complex and more like individual apartment buildings on a residential street. Two three-story buildings stood on each side of the road. Each had eighteen apartments. Since it was located on the outskirts of town, there was more than enough land for parking. Ryan parked close to the building, and they went through a door at the side of the building. They climbed the stairs and went down the hall to unit 206.

Brooke knocked on the door. Several seconds later, Jenny answered and invited them in. The place was tiny. It looked like a hotel room with a kitchen. They walked past the kitchen on their right. To the left was a bathroom. On the far wall to the right were sliding glass doors that led to a small balcony. Next to the glass doors was a television hanging on the wall. In front of the television was a reclining chair, and on the left wall was a sofa sleeper. A small desk stood next to the sofa. Jenny's laptop sat open on it.

"I know it's small, but it's all I can afford while I'm going to school," Jenny said.

"I lived with a roommate in college," Brooke said. "I would have loved my own place."

"Try living with your parents while going to school," Ryan said.

"Okay, I feel better now," Jenny said, and they all laughed.

"Do you have it?" Ryan asked.

Jenny pulled a thumb drive from her laptop and handed it to Ryan. "You know I could have emailed this to you."

"I know, but I thought it would be better if we talked about our next steps in person. Plus, we need to see someone else in the area."

Jenny picked up her laptop from the desk and invited them to sit on the sofa. She sat on the chair and set the computer on the coffee table. "I just learned that the general will return tomorrow afternoon for another demonstration," Jenny said.

"That was quick," Brooke said. "Will that interfere with what you call a plan, Ryan?"

"I was counting on the demonstration, but the time frame makes it difficult."

Jenny opened the laptop and used it to start a video call with Kevin Miller. They talked for about thirty minutes, discussing all their options. After they came up with a plan, Jenny disconnected with Kevin and asked, "Is anyone hungry? I have a frozen pizza I can put in the oven."

"Thanks, but we have another meeting, and my son is at the neighbor's house. Ethan's a good kid, but he's not their responsibility."

***

Once back in the car, Brooke asked, "So, who are we seeing next?"

"His name is Donald Marelli. Your friend Mary gave us some names of the investors in Jones's company. It was your idea, remember?"

"Of course, I remember. Did you research this guy? Do you think he can help us?"

"I think he can. He is the second-largest shareholder in the company. From what I've read, he has a significant amount of influence. When we show him what Jenny gave us, he might be willing to help, but there's no guarantee."

Donald Marelli had a large house in a rural area west of Gainesville. They stopped before a tall, wrought iron gate, and Ryan pushed the intercom button.

After several seconds, a voice said, "Can I help you?"

"It's Ryan Clark and Brooke McCabe here to see Donald Marelli."

After a few seconds, the gate slid open. The narrow driveway led Brooke and Ryan through a canopy of trees. When they emerged on the other side, the paved driveway had turned to bricks, which led to a large two-story home. The driveway formed a circle at the front of the house, with a fountain in the center.

Ryan parked in front of the house. They walked up the steps to a large set of double doors. Each door was made from fine mahogany. The wood formed tree branches in the center of each door, and stained glass filled in the gaps. The glass was arranged into colorful leaves and birds.

"This is beautiful," Brooke said as one of the doors opened.

An attractive blonde woman of about fifty came out to greet them. "Hi. I'm Silvia Marelli. Welcome."

Brooke and Ryan introduced themselves, and Silvia led them to the living room. It was a fairly large room with a leather sectional sofa in front of a fireplace that had no fire. It was probably only used in the winter. "Have a seat," Silvia said. "My husband is on an important call and will be out shortly."

Ryan sat at the far-left end of the sofa, and Brooke sat next to him. Silvia sat in the center and said, "Can I get you anything? Water? Soda?"

Ryan looked at Brooke, who shook her head. He said, "Thank you, Mrs. Marelli, but we're fine."

"Please, call me Silvia."

Mr. Marelli, a portly man of average height with thinning dark hair, entered the living room. Brooke and Ryan stood up, and they all introduced themselves. "It is so nice to meet you, Mr. Marelli," Ryan said.

"We are informal around here. You can call me Don," he said before sitting beside his wife.

"Okay, Don," Ryan said as he reached into his pocket and pulled out the thumb drive Jenny gave him. "We have evidence that the animals in the CJL genetics lab are being mistreated."

"What is that? What do you have?" Don asked.

Ryan held up the thumb drive. "There are videos on here taken by an employee with a hidden camera. There are laws in Florida covering the treatment of lab animals. If a regulator saw these, they would shut down your operation instantly."

"Let me see that," Don said as he stood and took the drive from Ryan's hand. He went into another room and returned with his laptop. He sat beside his wife again, inserted the drive into the computer, and played the first video. "They both watched in shock. After the last video finished, Silvia looked at her husband and said, "That woman is terrible. You need to show this to Jones and have her fired."

"That won't work," Brooke said. "Jones hired her knowing what she is like."

"So, what can I do?" Don asked.

"We hear you have a lot of influence with the board members. You need to remove Jones as CEO and get someone more compassionate to replace him."

"You're asking a lot. Jones has a higher stake in the company than I do."

"If he is not removed," Ryan said, "We will have no choice but to turn these videos over to the proper authorities. That will surely get your genetics operation shut down. In addition, once the press gets wind of it, public opinion of your company will go down the tubes. We don't want that, Don. We think your dogs have great potential as service animals, but not under the current conditions at that lab."

"Tell your stockholders that Dr. Miller will return, and nobody will see these recordings if they choose a new, more compassionate CEO," Brooke added.

Don Marelli sighed. "Okay, I'll see what I can do, but I make no promises."

While driving home after their meeting, Brooke asked, "If all of these crazy plans actually work, what then? I mean, what will become of Apollo and Athena?"

"I think creating dogs with that much intelligence comes with much responsibility. They can't be treated like pets or even service animals. They must be allowed to choose their destinies."

"I agree, but I can't imagine a dog like Apollo would refuse to work in the service of people who need it," Brooke said. "They are still dogs, after all."

"You have a good point."

They stopped first to pick up Ethan. When they arrived, Stacy met them at the door.

"Thank you so much for keeping an eye on Ethan," Ryan said. "I hope he wasn't too much trouble."

"Not at all. He's a good kid. Do you have any news about Apollo?"

"We have a plan to get him out of there tomorrow," Brooke said. "Of course, that depends on everything going perfectly."

"If you do manage to get him out, won't they just return here and take him back?"

"We have a plan for that, too," Ryan said.

"Well, I hope your plans work. Apollo was a real godsend for Ava. I mean, I know he will probably stay with you, but maybe he could hang out with Ava a couple of days a week."

"I think I have a better idea," Brooke said.

***

Jack Strauss didn't usually work on Sundays, but something Ryan Clark told him nagged at his heart. After dinner, he told his wife he had to go to the lab to check on something and that it wouldn't take long.

The building was darker than he was used to. It wasn't empty. There were always people there, but most areas were shut down for the weekend. He walked to the genetics lab and opened the door. It was mostly dark, with only a few lights illuminating the inside. He flipped the light switch near the door, and the entire room brightened.

He walked past the row of dog cages. Every dog was now awake. A couple of dogs barked, but the rest just watched Jack walk by. Athena stood as he passed. Next to her was an empty pen labeled "Apollo."

"Where's Apollo?" he asked out loud to no one in particular.

Athena barked.

"He's not still in that little cage, is he?"

Athena barked again.

"Apollo!" he called out. "Where are you?"

He heard several barks coming from the other side of the lab. He walked quickly and found Apollo still stuffed into the small cage. He opened the door, and Apollo came out, stretched, and barked once at Jack.

"I assume that means 'thank you.' You're welcome. I can't believe that woman left you in there. Let's go back to where you belong. Apollo followed Jack back to his normal pen next to Athena. Once inside, Jack closed the door, squatted to Apollo's eye level, and said, "If anyone asks, I wasn't here."

Chapter 13

Jenny arrived at the lab about an hour earlier than usual the next day. She wanted to be there well before Dr. Lopez arrived. Apollo was back in his regular pen next to Athena. Apparently, cooperating with Dr. Lopez got him out of the doghouse, so to speak.

"Apollo. I'm so glad that crazy Dr. Lopez put you back where you belong."

Apollo barked twice

"No? What does that mean?

Apollo barked.

"Never mind. It's great that you can understand, but I wish you could speak, too." She opened his pen and let him out. She then let Athena out. She didn't bother putting leashes on them. Instead, she took them out to the fenced-in training area.

The space was initially used as an outdoor break area, and it continued to serve that purpose. However, when the dogs required more room for training, Jones had a fence erected around the area.

A large, flat canopy extended about forty feet along the side of the building from the door to the fence. Four picnic tables stood end to end under the canopy, with several feet of open space between each table.

Jenny went over with Apollo and Athena what they would do after the general arrived. She also set up a new trick she wanted them to learn. Once she was sure they knew what to do, she brought the rest of the dogs out for their morning walk.

When Dr. Lopez arrived, she told Jenny to bring out Apollo and Athena so they could practice what they would do at the demonstration. Once outside, Jenny pointed out that she had already been practicing with the dogs and suggested that she should lead the demonstration, as she had developed a bond with them.

"That's fine," Lopez said, "but I don't want any screwups. This is way too important for me and the company."

***

Ryan called Brooke that morning and asked if she wanted to join them for breakfast. She said she would love to and would be there in half an hour. Forty-five minutes later, Ryan finished cooking the first pancake and set it in front of Ethan. He was about to start another one when the doorbell rang.

Ryan opened the door and saw Brooke standing there wearing tennis shoes, white shorts, and a pink T-shirt. She smiled and brushed her hair back as Ryan invited her inside.

"You look great," he said.

"Really?" she said as she looked down at her clothes. "I wasn't trying to look good. I wanted to dress comfortably today in case we have to move fast."

"We might have to drive fast, but if we have to get out and run, that would mean our plan went off the rails."

"Well, I figured better safe than sorry." Brooke sniffed the air. "Something smells good."

"I'm making pancakes," Ryan said, leading Brooke into the kitchen.

"Good morning, Ethan," she said as she entered the room.

Ethan swallowed his food. "Good morning, Brooke. Are you ready for today?"

"As ready as I'll ever be. What about you?"

"Are you kidding? I can't wait to see Apollo again."

Ryan had started cooking another pancake. He turned to Ethan and said, "There are no guarantees, Ethan. I told you this may not work, so don't get your hopes up."

"Too late," Ethan said, taking another bite of his pancake.

Ryan looked at Brooke and shook his head.

"It's fine," Brooke said. "There's nothing wrong with having a little hope."

"I suppose not. I just don't want to see him disappointed."

"If this doesn't work, we will all be disappointed," Brooke said. "There's not much you can do to change that."

"I suppose you're right about that, too," Ryan said as he flipped the pancake over.

When the pancake was finished, he put it on a plate and placed it in front of Brooke. He then cooked one for himself and joined them at the table. "I hope nobody was upset that you closed your clinic today."

Brooke was about to take a bite of her pancake, but put her fork down and said, "It was a light day today with no emergencies, so it shouldn't be a problem for anyone."

They hung around Ryan's house and talked until it was time to go. This time, Brooke drove her SUV. They arranged to meet Kevin Miller at eleven-thirty at a family restaurant about a mile from Charles Jones Laboratories. They didn't want to wait until the last minute and risk traffic delays.

They arrived five minutes early and were seated at a table. Kevin arrived a few minutes later and joined them. The demonstration was scheduled for one o'clock, so they ordered lunch and talked until twelve-thirty.

They then headed to Charles Jones Laboratories, parking their vehicles on the side of the road just outside the fenced-in area, out of sight of the guardhouse. Kevin's car was in front. He raised his hood so it would appear he was having engine trouble. He then joined Ethan in the back of the SUV.

Several minutes later, they watched a black sedan drive by. Kevin saw the general in the passenger seat and said, "That's them."

"I was expecting to see some kind of army vehicle," Ethan said.

"I'm sure the car he's in is more comfortable and uses less gas," Kevin said.

***

Charles Jones waited outside the front entrance as the car carrying General Adams and Captain Davis pulled up. A few seconds later, a limousine arrived, and Donald Marelli stepped out. They all converged at the same moment. "Welcome, General. Captain," Jones said. "This is one of our top investors, Donald Marelli."

Marelli shook the General's hand and then the Captain's. "I'm pleased to meet you both."

"Follow me," Jones said. "We have quite a show for you today."

They walked inside, passed the reception desk, and then passed the genetics lab before exiting out the back door to the demonstration area. Dr. Lopez, Jenny, Apollo, and Athena stood near the door to the right. Everyone shook hands, and then Dr. Lopez told Jenny to get started.

Jenny walked about five paces toward the center of the enclosed area and stopped. She turned, got down on one knee, and said, "Apollo. Athena. Were you two paying attention to everyone's names?"

Both dogs barked, and Jenny said, "Good. When I say 'go,' I want you, Apollo, to shake General Adams's hand, and I want you, Athena, to shake Captain Davis's hand. Go!"

Apollo walked to where General Adams stood, sat in front of him, and raised his right paw. Athena did the same thing to Captain Davis. They both shook their respective dog's paws. When they let go, everyone clapped. Everyone clapped except Jack Strauss, who, this time, decided to stand next to the exit with his tranquilizer gun ready.

Apollo and Athena returned to Jenny, who told them she was proud of them. She then took several stuffed animals out of a bag and lined them up on the ground about six inches apart. The assortment included a cat, a dog, a bear, an elephant, a snake, a rabbit, and a pig. She said, "Athena, pick up the pig and bring it to Mr. Jones."

Athena picked up the pig, walked over to Charles Jones, and dropped it at his feet. She then returned and sat next to Apollo.

"Apollo," Jenny said," Bring the snake to Dr. Lopez."

Apollo picked up the snake, brought it to Dr. Lopez, and dropped it at her feet.

General Adams turned to Captain Davis and whispered, "I wonder if she was sending them a subtle message."

Captain Davis smiled but said nothing.

When Apollo returned, Jenny said, "You are both doing great. Now, give me your right paw."

Apollo lifted his right paw for Jenny, who took it in her hand and said, "Very good, Apollo."

She let go of his paw and turned to Athena. "Athena, give me your left paw."

Athena lifted her left paw. Jenny took it in both hands and said, "Good girl."

Jenny glanced at her watch and then looked over at Jack Strauss, who was standing near the gate. She didn't expect him to stand there. He could ruin everything, but she was committed. There was no plan B. "Now, we will show you their agility and balance," she told the audience.

There were two stepladders folded and leaning against the wall. She opened one under the awning and dragged it out a few feet. She opened the other and placed it several feet away from the first. She then placed a wooden board between the two ladders.

"Okay, Apollo and Athena," she said. "I want you to climb up the ladder, walk across the board, and climb down the other side. Do you understand?"

They both barked.

**

When the time arrived, Kevin returned to his car and drove to the gate. The man at the guard station recognized him when he opened his window.

"Dr. Miller. It's good to see you again. Did you get your old job back?"

"No, I'm afraid not. I have an appointment to see Jenny Smith."

The man looked at his clipboard. "Oh. I see you here. Okay, Dr. Miller. Have a nice day." He pushed a button, and the gate slowly slid open.

When the gate finished moving, Kevin pulled ahead slowly until his car was partway through the gate, and then he killed the engine. The man stepped out of the guard shack and said, "What's wrong, Dr. Miller?"

"I don't know," Kevin said, pretending to push the start button. "It just died. Now it won't start. It won't even try to start."

"Pop the hood, the security guard said."

Kevin popped the hood and got out of the car. The two men looked at the engine. "Well," the security guard said. "It looks like your battery cables are connected securely. I don't know what it could be. Perhaps you should call a tow truck. In the meantime, we should push it out of the way."

Kevin looked behind him and then at his watch. "Can we give it a couple of minutes? This happened once before, a couple of weeks ago. After a short time, it started right back up. Nobody's coming. If a car does come, we can push it away then."

The security guard looked down the road and said, "Okay, I guess five minutes wouldn't hurt."

***

Apollo ascended the ladder with Athena close behind. Once at the top, he slowly walked across the board until he reached the second ladder. He looked back. Athena was close behind him. Instead of going down the second ladder, he leaped onto the awning. Athena jumped and landed behind Apollo.

Everyone but Jenny had a shocked look on their faces. "Hey! Hey! Stop them! Stop them!" Jones yelled.

Jack Straus watched the two dogs heading in his direction. He took out his tranquilizer gun and aimed it at Apollo. He waited for him to get close. He didn't want to risk missing, as his tranquilizer pistol needed to be reloaded after each shot. As the dogs got closer, Jack's grip on the trigger tightened. Then Apollo stopped. He sat down, looked Jack in the eyes, and raised his right paw."

Jack loosened his grip on the trigger. Athena sat down and also raised her right paw in the air. Jack sighed and lowered the gun. Apollo and Athena continued running across the awning and jumped to the ground on the other side of the fence. After hitting the soft grass, Apollo turned and barked once at Jack. He and Athena then raced to the main gate.

Jones reached Jack and said, "What's the matter with you? Why didn't you shoot?"

"They asked me not to," Jack said.

"What do you mean they asked you not to? What are you talking about? Never mind. Give me the gun."

Jones tried to take the gun, but Jack was faster and pulled it away. "I think now is a good time to tender my resignation," Jack said.

"Are you serious? What's going on around here?"

Kevin saw Apollo and Athena from a distance. He said, "I think it might be okay now." He closed the hood and got into the car.

He started the engine and gave the guard a thumbs-up. "It's working now," he said as Apollo and Athena ran past his car. This time, nobody was in pursuit.

The security guard came out of his booth as Kevin backed away. "Dr. Miller! Where are you going?" Kevin watched him put his hands on his head in disbelief as his car reached the road.

Ethan was waiting outside Brooke's SUV when Apollo and Athena approached. Apollo excitedly put his front legs on Ethan's shoulder and licked his face. "I'm happy to see you, too, Buddy."

"Get in the car! We have to go now!" Ryan yelled.

Everyone piled into the vehicle. Ethan sat in the middle, with Apollo on his left and Athena on his right. As soon as his seatbelt was on, Brooke made a quick U-turn and raced away from Charles Jones Laboratories, with Kevin following close behind.

They drove straight home without stopping. When they got close, Brooke's phone rang. She didn't recognize the number but answered it and put it on speaker. "Hello," she said.

"Is this Brooke McCabe?" asked the male voice on the other end.

"Yes. This is she."

"This is General Adams. I got your letter. To be honest, when you said I should negotiate with you instead of Charles Jones, I thought you were a crackpot. I have much respect for your brother. He is confident and has the intelligence to back it up. I can tell you two are siblings."

"Thank you, General," Brooke said. "Are you still interested in dogs for the army?"

"I'm even more interested now. You could have only pulled off that escape if those dogs knew your plan beforehand. They really are amazing."

"Yes, they are, but they're not war dogs. They're service dogs. If you want dogs like Apollo and Athena, you must agree that they will only be used as service dogs for military veterans who need them."

The General sighed, "As much as I would like to see these dogs helping our combat troops, I know it is equally important to support our veterans. I'm just not convinced that you are the person I should negotiate with. What stake do you have in all this?"

Brooke looked at Ryan and smiled. "Why don't we talk more tomorrow, General? I think everything will be clearer then."

Chapter 14

Ryan bought steaks in anticipation of a victory. He even prepared steak for Apollo and Athena. Jenny was also there after walking off the job. During dinner, Ryan's phone rang. He left it in the kitchen and got up to answer it. After listening to the caller, he said, "Thanks so much for letting me know."

Just as he sat back down at the table, the doorbell rang. He got back up and answered the door. A sheriff's deputy stood there with Charles Jones behind him. "I'm sorry, sir, but the dogs you are harboring will have to come with me," the officer said.

"By whose authority?" Ryan asked.

"By my authority," Jones said. "They're my dogs."

"They don't belong to anybody!" Ethan yelled.

Ryan turned around and saw that everyone, including Apollo and Athena, had gotten up from the table and now stood behind him. He turned back to the officer and said, "The CEO of Charles Jones Laboratories allowed me to keep these dogs."

"Don't listen to him," Jones said to the officer. "I'm the CEO of the company."

"I think you need to talk to someone," Ryan said, taking out his phone. He dialed a number. When it was answered, he said, "Charles Jones is at my house right now." After a few seconds, Ryan said, "Okay," and tapped the speaker button.

He held the phone out and said, "It's Donald Marelli."

Jones sighed, "What is it, Don? I'm busy here."

"We've been trying to reach you. After the fiasco today and the videos we got of animal abuse . . ."

"Abuse? What abuse?"

"If you don't know what is happening in your own company, that confirms our decision was correct."

"Decision? What decision? What are you getting at, Don?"

"The board decided to remove you from the CEO position effective immediately. I will serve as interim CEO until we find a permanent replacement. You have also been removed as Chairman of the Board."

"You can't replace me. It's my company."

"You might have started the company, but you would have never been successful without the help of investors like me. I'm afraid the board has already voted. You still have an ownership interest but no longer run the company."

The officer interrupted, saying, "I need to know what to do about the dogs."

"The dogs are fine where they are," Marelli said.

"Okay, then," he said. "Have a good night, everyone."

As the officer turned and started walking down the stairs, Jenny stepped forward and said, "It was a pleasure to see you again, Mr. Jones. Have a good night."

Jones looked as though he wanted to say something, but he turned and walked down the stairs instead. Ryan closed the door and turned around. Everyone looked at each other briefly and then broke out into laughter.

After dinner was over and the dishes were cleaned, Kevin and Jenny left for home. Ryan looked at Ethan and said, "You should take Apollo and Athena outside to do their business."

"Okay, but we only have one leash."

"Don't worry about the leash. Just stay close to home."

After Ethan left with the dogs, Brooke stepped close to Ryan and said, "I've been waiting for a quiet time to talk to you. When I told you I didn't want to get involved in a relationship, that was me trying to protect myself from pain."

"It's okay, Ryan said. "I understand. You don't have to explain."

"Please, let me finish. I saw today how teamwork and taking risks can lead to something extraordinary. I've been doing the opposite. I've been trying to do everything myself while avoiding risks entirely. To be honest, it's not working. I haven't been happy. Sure, I'm good at putting on a happy face, but..."

"What are you saying, exactly?"

Brooke leaned in and kissed Ryan. She pulled away and said, "I'm saying that I'm willing to take a chance on you if you'll still have me."

Ryan kissed Brooke. This time, nobody pulled away.

**

Two months later, Ryan, Brooke, Ethan, and Apollo were eating breakfast when the doorbell rang. Brooke answered the door and saw Kevin standing there. "Kevin, come on in."

Apollo rushed to the door to greet him. Kevin knelt and hugged him as he licked his face. Ethan got up from the table and hurried to his bedroom. He came out holding a notebook. "I'm ready for you, Dr. Kevin."

Kevin stood and said, "Let me see what you have."

Ethan handed him his notebook. Kevin flipped through the pages and said, "Very good, Ethan. You're going to be a great scientist one day."

"I never go to bed without first writing about what Apollo learned that day."

Kevin read some of the entries and said, "It looks like you taught him a lot of new words this week. You even have a couple of Spanish words in here."

"Just hola and adios. They're the only Spanish words I know."

"How is his retention? I mean, does he remember the words you taught him last week?"

"He forgets sometimes, but his memory is better than mine."

Kevin handed the notebook to Ethan and said, "Keep up the good work, and don't forget to email those pages to me."

"I won't," Ethan said, returning the notebook to his bedroom.

Kevin turned his attention to Brooke and Ryan, saying, "By the way, I got your wedding invitation yesterday and wanted to congratulate you both."

"Thank you, Kevin," Brooke said. "What about you? How do you like working back at the lab?"

"Oh, it's so much better now. Our new CEO started last week and is very supportive. She's also an animal lover. I couldn't be happier. Jenny's back in school, so she's not around as much, but I manage. Oh, we also have our first litter of puppies. If all goes well, they will be the first to help our veterans needing service animals once they are older and trained."

"I'm sure they will be very helpful," Ryan said. "Speaking of helpful, how are Athena and Ava doing?"

"I saw them yesterday, and they have both settled into the college routine quite nicely. Athena knows exactly where all of Ava's classes are. She also knows how to get to the bus stop and the local food mart. Ava probably also goes to other places that she doesn't tell me about."

"I'm sure that's true. We are so happy everything worked out with her," Brooke said. "How's her vision? Has it improved at all?"

"Actually, it has. She's able to make out shapes now. Her doctors are optimistic about her future, but she still has a long road ahead of her."

"That's good news," Brooke said.

"How's your new book coming, Ryan?" Kevin asked.

"Great. I finished the first draft a few days ago. I'm calling it 'Saving Apollo.' My editor thinks it will be a hit. It's my first non-fiction book, so I'm a little nervous about it."

"I will certainly buy it," Kevin said.

"I'm looking forward to reading it, too," Brooke said, "even though I know how it ends."

"Well, I just came to check on Apollo," Kevin said. "I should get going now."

"Already?" Brooke asked. "Would you like to stay for breakfast? You must be hungry."

"No, thank you. I picked up a bagel on the way here. Besides, I need to get home. I have a demanding cat I haven't paid much attention to all week."

"I know what that's like," Brooke said.

When Kevin got home, he took off his shoes, sat on the sofa, and put his feet up on the coffee table. A Siamese cat jumped onto the sofa and curled up on his lap. Kevin petted the cat and said, "How's it going, Milo?"

"Fine," Milo said. "How was your visit with Apollo?"

"It went very well. Apollo is progressing better than we ever imagined."

"That's good. I knew you would find a way to make dogs almost as smart as cats."

I truly appreciate you taking the time to read Saving Apollo. I hope you enjoyed the story.

I would be incredibly grateful if you left a review on Amazon, Goodreads, or wherever you purchased this book. Your thoughts help other readers discover my books and mean a lot to me as an author. Whether it's a few words or a detailed review, your feedback makes a difference.

Thank you again for your support. I couldn't do this without readers like you.

Charles Huss

Books by Charles Huss

Last Healer Mysteries Series

Joe, a reclusive, ageless Centenarian, meets Katie, an ambitious news personality with dreams of being an investigative reporter. Together, they solve crimes and explore the full potential of Joe's healing abilities while navigating the complexities of their intimate relationship.

The Last Healer

On the eve of her thirtieth birthday, Katie, a television news reporter, unhappy with her career and her love life, decides to spend the weekend alone at a Wisconsin ski resort.

Joe is a man content to live a private life in his cabin in the woods. Since the death of his wife, he has avoided intimate relationships and prefers to keep a low profile to prevent people from learning of his unusual abilities.

On the way to the ski resort, Katie makes a wrong turn during a snowstorm and hits Joe with her car. Lost and with no cell signal, Katie tries to keep Joe alive until she can get help. During Joe's recovery, Katie learns his secret and soon helps to investigate his family's mysterious past while Joe helps Katie investigate a double murder. Love blossoms while they slowly unravel both mysteries, but danger lies ahead. Can Joe discover the full extent of his abilities before it is too late?

Last Rites

In this gripping sequel to "The Last Healer," Katie and Joe, fresh from their honeymoon, must race to Milwaukee to save the life of Katie's dear friend Ashley after she and her mother fall victim to a ruthless attack. With Ashley on the brink of death, while a priest delivers Last Rites, her only chance for survival is Joe's remarkable healing powers.

What starts as a rescue mission turns into a murder investigation as they investigate the killing of Ashley's mother. While searching for the shooter, their investigation leads them to a chilling conspiracy centered on the city's homeless population. As they uncover more of the truth, they become targets as someone is determined to silence them. Will Katie and Joe find who is behind a series of murders, or will they become the next victims?

Last Chance

In Book Three of the Last Healer Mysteries, Katie and Joe, after deciding to quit investigating murders, are thrust back into it when a man is murdered at Joe's resort.

The victim is no ordinary man. He is a suspected jewel thief, believed to have hidden stolen jewels at the resort. While they struggle to handle all the treasure seekers, Katie and Joe debate how involved they should be in the murder investigation. They don't know the killer lurks in the background, taking orders from some of the most powerful people in Wisconsin while he waits for Katie and Joe to find what he is looking for.

Last Flight

In Book Four of the Last Healer Mysteries series, Katie and Joe witness the deadly crash of a prototype aircraft and save the life of one of its occupants. After Joe discovers evidence of sabotage, Katie insists she can investigate the crime despite being almost nine months pregnant.

Someone planted an explosive device in the aircraft, killing the company's founder and jeopardizing the struggling startup's future. Was the attack meant to destroy the company, or was it something more personal? As Katie and Joe hit one dead end after another, they discover the killer isn't finished. With time running out, they race to save the next victim, but with people dying, a murderer on the loose, and Katie in labor, what's a Healer to do?

Last Hope

In the fifth Last Healer Mystery, Katie and Joe learn of a tragedy in Katie's hometown while they are celebrating their son's first birthday. The husband of Katie's childhood best friend stands accused of murdering the community's lone police detective. They return to the small Wisconsin town, determined to find the real killer.

As they dig deeper, they uncover chilling ties between the detective's death and the recent killing of the mayor's daughter. It soon becomes clear someone will stop at nothing to keep the truth buried.

Truth Be Told

Peter Beckett awoke 25 years ago with no memory of his past. Since then, he's been haunted by a gift he never asked for and doesn't want. People can't lie to him. To Peter, it feels like a curse that has left him isolated and feared by all who get to know him. Only his priest accepts him for who he is.

The FBI has been watching him, and they need his unique talent to track a deadly drug cartel that has infiltrated Milwaukee, fueling a dangerous spike of fentanyl overdoses. Rookie agent Hannah Meyers is assigned to recruit Peter, who is reluctant to help, but is intrigued by Hannah after she lies to him.

As the investigation deepens, details of Peter's former life emerge. With secrets unraveling and lives on the line, Peter must decide whether to return to the glorious life he once knew or give it all up for love.

Identity Crisis

After Alex Neumann agrees to participate in his father's groundbreaking memory recording experiment, he awakens years later to find he is not the man he used to be. He soon becomes a pawn in a deadly scheme involving a ruthless businessman, an Army general, and the President of The United States.

As Alex peels away layers of deception, his true identity slowly emerges, along with skills foreign to his old self. He will need all those skills and the help of friends he meets along the way to survive and turn the tables on his adversaries.

Falling Star

A meteorite crashes into the serene wilderness of a national park. In its aftermath, both people and animals succumb to aggressive behavior followed by death. Two rookies, FBI agent Beth Hartley and Park Ranger Mike Bauer, are put together to investigate the strange events.

Beth is tough as they come on the outside but vulnerable on the inside. After her last breakup, she has given up on men to focus on her career. Mike, a former military police officer, has developed trust issues and prefers his new career where he has no partner that he needs to rely on.

As their investigation brings them closer to the truth, they find themselves getting closer to each other. In a dangerous forest where every animal is a potential threat, and even the air could be toxic, their best chance for survival is a partner they can trust.

Bad Cat Chris: The Baddest Cat You'll Ever Love

When Chuck volunteered to help a local cat shelter clean cages one morning, the last thing he expected was a kitten climbing up his back to perch on his shoulders, but that was the beginning of a relationship that would test the limits of human endurance and compassion.

This is the story of Chris, a cat like no other who would turn the lives of Chuck and Rose upside-down while eventually showing them that bad can be good and love can come from the most unlikely places.

This book is based on Chris's blog at BadCatChris.com and is a collection of sometimes serious but mostly humorous stories about the ups and downs of living with a bad cat.

About The Author

Charles Huss was born and raised in the suburbs of Chicago but has lived most of his adult life in the Tampa Bay, Florida, area. He is a graduate of St. Petersburg College and is the author of several books. He currently lives with his wife, Rose, and their two cats.

Don't miss out!

Visit the website below and you can sign up to receive emails whenever Charles Huss publishes a new book. There's no charge and no obligation.

https://books2read.com/r/B-A-LHRY-UKPGG

Connecting independent readers to independent writers.

Did you love *Saving Apollo*? Then you should read *The Last Healer*[1] by Charles Huss!

[2]

On the eve of her thirtieth birthday, Katie, a television news reporter, unhappy with her career and her love life, decides to spend the weekend alone at a Wisconsin ski resort.

Joe is a man content to live a private life in his cabin in the woods. Since the death of his wife, he has avoided intimate relationships and prefers to keep a low profile to prevent people from learning of his unusual abilities.

On the way to the ski resort, Katie makes a wrong turn during a snowstorm and hits Joe with her car. Lost and with no cell signal, Katie tries to keep Joe alive until she can get help. During Joe's recovery, Katie learns his secret and soon helps to investigate his family's mysterious

---

1. https://books2read.com/u/3yQJ0B

2. https://books2read.com/u/3yQJ0B

past while Joe helps Katie investigate a double murder. Love blossoms while they slowly unravel both mysteries, but danger lies ahead. Can Joe discover the full extent of his abilities before it is too late?

The Last Healer is part mystery, part romance, and part science fiction. It is a book that can be enjoyed in just a few hours but remembered for a lifetime.

Read more at charleshuss.com.